He was still alive. For now

Footsteps sounded on both sides of him as his attackers charged through the brush. The sound was deafening, rhythmic. It was the sound of his own death trampling over the ground.

Bolan felt like a trapped creature of prey. His heart was pounding and blood was pumping too rapidly in his skull, and he realized he'd been holding his breath. The near-death experience had thrown him off his game. His instinct was to run from the dead zone, but that would be suicide. If he scrambled to his feet now he'd be put down forever. All those thoughts flooded through his mind in a fraction of a second—but in combat a second was an eternity.

And it was long enough for the Executioner to calculate his best move.

MACK BOLAN ®
The Executioner

#200 Crisis Point
#201 Prime Target
#202 Combat Zone
#203 Hard Contact
#204 Rescue Run
#205 Hell Road
#206 Hunting Cry
#207 Freedom Strike
#208 Death Whisper
#209 Asian Crucible
#210 Fire Lash
#211 Steel Claws
#212 Ride the Beast
#213 Blood Harvest
#214 Fission Fury
#215 Fire Hammer
#216 Death Force
#217 Fight or Die
#218 End Game
#219 Terror Intent
#220 Tiger Stalk
#221 Blood and Fire
#222 Patriot Gambit
#223 Hour of Conflict
#224 Call to Arms
#225 Body Armor
#226 Red Horse
#227 Blood Circle
#228 Terminal Option
#229 Zero Tolerance
#230 Deep Attack
#231 Slaughter Squad
#232 Jackal Hunt
#233 Tough Justice
#234 Target Command
#235 Plague Wind
#236 Vengeance Rising
#237 Hellfire Trigger

#238 Crimson Tide
#239 Hostile Proximity
#240 Devil's Guard
#241 Evil Reborn
#242 Doomsday Conspiracy
#243 Assault Reflex
#244 Judas Kill
#245 Virtual Destruction
#246 Blood of the Earth
#247 Black Dawn Rising
#248 Rolling Death
#249 Shadow Target
#250 Warning Shot
#251 Kill Radius
#252 Death Line
#253 Risk Factor
#254 Chill Effect
#255 War Bird
#256 Point of Impact
#257 Precision Play
#258 Target Lock
#259 Nightfire
#260 Dayhunt
#261 Dawnkill
#262 Trigger Point
#263 Skysniper
#264 Iron Fist
#265 Freedom Force
#266 Ultimate Price
#267 Invisible Invader
#268 Shattered Trust
#269 Shifting Shadows
#270 Judgment Day
#271 Cyberhunt
#272 Stealth Striker
#273 UForce
#274 Rogue Target
#275 Crossed Borders

DON PENDLETON'S
EXECUTIONER®
THE
CROSSED BORDERS

A GOLD EAGLE BOOK FROM
WORLDWIDE®

TORONTO • NEW YORK • LONDON
AMSTERDAM • PARIS • SYDNEY • HAMBURG
STOCKHOLM • ATHENS • TOKYO • MILAN
MADRID • WARSAW • BUDAPEST • AUCKLAND

First edition October 2001
ISBN 0-373-64275-X

Special thanks and acknowledgment to
Rich Rainey for his contribution to this work.

CROSSED BORDERS

Get your facts first, and then you can distort them as much as you please.

—Mark Twain

As nightfall does not come at once, neither does oppression. In both instances, there's a twilight where everything remains seemingly unchanged, and it is in such twilight that we must be aware of change in the air, however slight, lest we become unwitting victims of the darkness.

—Supreme Court Justice William O. Douglas

The drug war is an illusion spun by politicians addicted to office.

—Mack Bolan

THE
MACK BOLAN
LEGEND

Nothing less than a war could have fashioned the destiny of the man called Mack Bolan. Bolan earned the Executioner title in the jungle hell of Vietnam.

But this soldier also wore another name—Sergeant Mercy. He was so tagged because of the compassion he showed to wounded comrades-in-arms and Vietnamese civilians.

Mack Bolan's second tour of duty ended prematurely when he was given emergency leave to return home and bury his family, victims of the Mob. Then he declared a one-man war against the Mafia.

He confronted the Families head-on from coast to coast, and soon a hope of victory began to appear. But Bolan had broken society's every rule. That same society started gunning for this elusive warrior—to no avail.

So Bolan was offered amnesty to work within the system against terrorism. This time, as an employee of Uncle Sam, Bolan became Colonel John Phoenix. With a command center at Stony Man Farm in Virginia, he and his new allies—Able Team and Phoenix Force—waged relentless war on a new adversary: the KGB.

But when his one true love, April Rose, died at the hands of the Soviet terror machine, Bolan severed all ties with Establishment authority.

Now, after a lengthy lone-wolf struggle and much soul-searching, the Executioner has agreed to enter an "arm's-length" alliance with his government once more, reserving the right to pursue personal missions in his Everlasting War.

1

Del Rio Sector, Texas Border

The NSA spooks watched the rendezvous from a half mile away, safely hidden from the Special Ops Border Patrol unit and the Mexican *federales*. They saw everything in close-up, thanks to the surveillance web tasked to this stretch of border. Military satellites and a high-altitude Unmanned Aerial Vehicle fed a constant stream of bird's-eye imagery to the two-man observation post that was shrouded beneath desert-colored netting.

One of the men watched real-time surveillance footage as it streamed across the tripod-mounted black box screens.

The other man, the pilot of the UAV, controlled the drone's visual path with a remote-control unit that resembled a million-dollar video game. He also controlled several cameras onboard the UAV, including a 900 mm piece that could zoom in for head shots of the target.

Right now the target was the leader of the Quintana Roo cartel, Jorge Macedonio, a man on the wanted list of every country in Central America. A man about to be delivered to the hands of the U.S. government.

"Here he comes," the pilot said.

EVEN WITH HIS HANDS cuffed behind his back and a short-barreled Heckler & Koch MP-5 pointed at his neck, Jorge

Macedonio still looked as if *he* were in command of the unit that escorted him toward the waiting Americans.

Nearly a head taller than the moving gauntlet of Mexican police, the bronze-skinned prisoner walked up the sandy ravine with a surefooted gait. He ignored the jeers of the heavily armed escort and looked straight ahead into the dark future he'd mapped for himself.

According to the deal worked out with the American authorities, this desolate stretch of borderland was to be his Golgotha. The end of his twenty-year reign.

The previously untouchable *narcotrafficante* had negotiated his surrender to the U.S. border unit shortly after his protector in the Ministry of Defense was accidentally shot in back of the head. Moments after the "accident" several competing cartel leaders put a price on Macedonio's head.

Now he was the second major Mexican trafficker to turn himself in. A month earlier another cartel chief had done the same thing, almost at this very same spot. A safe bed behind bars was preferable to a bullet in the head.

As he neared the top of the ravine, Macedonio scanned the ranks of the welcoming party that stood like sentinels on the ridge.

The Americans were silhouetted against the sun like birds on a wire, looking down at the procession of *federales*. The procession stretched all the way down to the flats by the river where the convoy of Mexican army and police vehicles had crossed. The high suspension vehicles with their outsized tires were already dried off and baking in the sun.

It was one of the shallowest stretches of the Rio Grande. At times it was almost possible to walk across the river without getting wet, using the smooth rocks as steppingstones. Drug traffickers and illegal alien parties did so with regularity. It happened all along that Del Rio sector, which had two hundred miles of remote ranch land bordering the river. Two hundred miles of an endless sieve pouring cocaine and contraband into the heart of America.

CAPTAIN ERNEST THOMAS watched the parade from the front of his BP special, a Border Patrol vehicle rigged for fast pursuit in desert terrain. He sat on the blunt-nosed hood, his binoculars focused on the tall man with his hands behind his back, thinking it was a good thing the man's hands were bound. This was a strong one. A cut above the usual cartel thug who depended upon firepower instead of muscle to intimidate his followers.

"How's he look?"

Thomas turned briefly toward the voice, which belonged to Michael Souther, a DEA agent who'd been after Macedonio for the past three years. Souther looked more like a trafficker than the drug dealers themselves with his thick mustache, thick arms folded across his chest and an even thicker head.

For some reason Souther still assumed he had some say in the operation. He'd attached himself to Thomas like a Sunday-morning hangover ever since they'd gathered on the ridge. Another unwanted adviser who wanted to run the show, Thomas thought.

Before turning the glasses back on Macedonio, Thomas gave the DEA man the kind of look that sent most of the captain's men into hiding to question their sanity for interrupting him while he was concentrating.

But Souther stood there immune, his arms folded across his chest. He was one of a matched set of five DEA agents who'd come to the party. A bunch of cynical hardasses, Thomas thought, almost as bad as his own people. The DEA unit had caught more traffickers than they could count, only to have the Agency or the Justice Department call them "assets" and set them free.

Business as usual, Thomas thought. One branch of the

government swatted the drug peddlers while another branch brushed them off, gave them Get Out of Jail Free cards and stuffed a wad of traveling money in their pockets.

Along with Souther's DEA crew, several other law-enforcement personnel swelled the ranks of his border interdiction unit today.

A flock of FBI agents stood around in rigid poses, looking like college professors about to lecture the rest of the group on how to catch criminals. Dark-suited vultures, Thomas thought, looking for a chance to swoop in on the spoils.

A group of U.S. Marshals was also standing by. Capping it off was a trio of spooks from D.C. who kept pretty much to themselves.

Everybody wanted credit on this one.

"You must be mad at me or something," Souther said.

"You must be psychic," Thomas growled. "How'd you guess?"

"Because you didn't answer me when I asked you how our man looked."

"You still want to know?"

"Sure."

The captain lowered his glasses. "He looks like a million dollars," he said.

"That's too bad," Souther replied. "The price on his head was two million."

"Maybe he's having a bad day."

"Considering what he's giving up, I guess he's entitled to that."

As Macedonio crested the lip of the ravine, Thomas unclipped his belt radio and thumbed it on as he held it in front of his mouth. "He's all yours, Lieutenant Almeida," he said. "Take that high and mighty son of a bitch into custody."

Flanked by two of his men, Almeida stepped to the edge of the ridge and reached out to grab Macedonio's shoulder.

Suddenly the prisoner opened fire.

Macedonio's hands whipped out from behind his back, each one holding a double-action SIG-Sauer P-226 pistol. He moved in a blur, shooting the officers on both sides of Almeida before aiming the barrels straight ahead and drilling the lieutenant with a point-blank barrage.

The 9 mm parabellum rounds climbed up through his breastbone and exploded out through the back of his neck. His head wobbled on the remnants of its spinal cord, and then he dropped down into the ravine.

The prisoner kept firing.

So did the police escort that brought him. Their Heckler & Koch MP-5 submachine guns raked across the line of fatally surprised lawmen, killing half of them before they realized what was happening.

A sniper, who'd crawled up the ridge, took out Captain Thomas with one shot to the head, exploding it like a melon all over the hood of his vehicle. He squeezed off a second shot that ripped through Souther's shoulder and smashed through the side window of the Border Patrol pursuit vehicle.

Souther spun, grasping his mangled shoulder as the blood spouted up through his fingers. Another shot cored through his gut and thunked into the chassis behind him. He fell to his knees as the blood pumped out of him in pulsing pools of red. Then he rested his head on the blood slicked door panel and stared at the slaughter taking place around him.

While the *federale* impostors raked the Americans with a withering fire that toppled blood-spattered bodies to the ground, the vehicles on the flats roared into life. They climbed up the hilly terrain on both sides of the ravine, carrying more gunners to the turkey shoot.

It was like ants pouring out of an anthill. Full-auto fire echoed up and down the ridge, punctuated now and then by the screams of the dead and the dying.

The sudden attack was so overwhelming that only a handful of men among the stunned Americans managed to return fire. They dropped to the ground or crouched behind their vehicles to take aim at the attacking force pouring over the lip of the ravine.

One of the hillside attackers stopped dead in his tracks when his Heckler & Koch clicked empty. As a stationary figure amid the chaos, he became the target of choice.

Four rounds hit him in the chest and legs and knocked him back down the ravine. Two other men in Mexican police uniforms were killed by the dwindling members of the border interdiction force.

But then the armor-piercing rounds ripped through the sides of the cars and SUVs and chewed through the bodies of the last defenders.

THE TWO MEN in the NSA observation post were hypnotized by the bloody images that appeared on their screens. It was happening too fast for them to comprehend, like something out of a horror movie. One moment their brethren were standing at attention, waiting to receive the gift horse of Jorge Macedonio. The next moment they were being cut down by Macedonio himself. By police officers. By army troops. All of them swarming up over the ridge.

The Americans were easy prey, thinking this handoff would go down just like the one last month. Mexican officials would deliver the prisoner. Smiles would break out all around. Lots of handshaking and chest thumping. Then all the parties could go home and tell the world what a wonderful job they're doing fighting the drug war.

But this time the Americans weren't going home.

"Jesus Christ," said the man piloting the camera as the horrific images came through. "What the hell's going on down there?"

"A massacre," the other man said, getting to his feet. "A bloody massacre. We've got to get down there."

"What can we do? There's only two of us. There's no way we can stop them."

"We can try—"

"No," the camera pilot said. He grabbed the other man's arm and tugged him back down to the ground. "We'll die if we go down there."

"But we have to do something!"

"Right," the pilot replied. "We have to do something that counts." He maneuvered the high-altitude camera to make another pass over the battlefield, then zoomed in on the faces of the murderers on the ridge. "Best thing we can do right now is track those bastards and have something to hand to someone who can do something about it."

THE MEN in Mexican police and army uniforms walked among the fallen Americans, collecting the spoils of war. Government IDs, badges and billfolds, passports, credit cards and state-of-the-art weapons. Now and then a shot rang out as they administered a coup de grâce to finish off a wounded man.

Although the uniforms were real, the soldiers and police were not. They handled themselves like military men, but their army wasn't recognized by any country in the Western Hemisphere.

Not yet.

That would come. The man who had posed as Jorge Macedonio would see that soon enough. He took off his sunglasses to look over the battlefield, adding yet another victory to his name.

He ran a hand through his dyed black hair, part of his carefully applied disguise. It was slick and parted in the middle and combed straight back in a braided war lock that ran down his shoulders.

Though he had approximately the same stature as the headman of the Quintana Roo cartel, Simon Liege had a hardness about him that the feared Mexican leader could never possess. It came from thirty years of making war across the globe for his country or for himself. Sometimes formally, sometimes covertly. Always to the maximum.

As a result, Liege had a reputation that attracted the best soldiers to his banner. He also had a failed marriage and two children in London who didn't know a thing about him. And he had a mistress in Belize who would probably betray him one day, with good reason. On top of all that, he'd suffered the loss of his right eye, which was replaced by an expensive glass orb that reflected the coldness of his heart.

And there were other injuries he'd gathered along the way, including badly healed fractures, bullet wounds, pins in his knees and one elbow, damaged nerves that periodically racked his body with pain. Most days pain was a constant with Liege. But so was pride. It was the life he chose and even with all the personal and physical sacrifices, he could conceive of no other life worth living.

After all, he was a soldier. A fighting man who made his own war if there were none to be found.

Unlike the real Macedonio who survived on sheer ruthlessness and an inbred brutality that made his own people fear him, Simon Liege knew how to exploit the other side's weakness. In this case the weakness was a thirst for victory. The Americans wanted a propaganda success to trumpet to the world and justify the hundreds of millions of dollars they squandered on an unwinnable drug war.

Liege gave them what they wanted. Jorge Macedonio. After making a trial run with the first surrender a month ago to study their procedures, it was a simple matter to plan their destruction with a second surrender.

Now the Americans paid the ultimate price for their predictability, and Liege had won the propaganda battle. The real Jorge Macedonio, one of his cartel clients, was the paymaster for this operation. When word got around, the other clients would fall in line. They'd been waiting to see if he could pull off a successful attack on American soil.

For too long the Americans had blindly waged war against the cartels, subverting their laws and seeking them out in their own countries. Now the war was coming home to them.

A man in a Mexican army uniform came running up to Liege. "One of the DEA men is still alive," he said. "Over there." He nodded toward the Border Patrol vehicle where the dead captain was sprawled on the hood.

Arturo Sandor stood by the vehicle, looking down and mocking a wounded man who was propped up against the door. Sandor was a colonel in the Mexican army who'd been forced to retire when his trafficking activities became too blatant even for his corrupt superiors.

Although the ex-colonel was a talented soldier, he had a streak of cruelty that could prove contagious among the newer soldiers. But he and his comrades still had a lot of influence in the critical provinces in Mexico, stretching from the northern border with the U.S. down to the Caribbean coast above Belize. That was the corridor of power through which Liege would build his army.

Sandor had to be handled.

Liege headed toward the wounded man and got there just in time to hear the ex-colonel taunting him about saving a bullet by waiting around to watch him die. The agonizing wounds would kill him slowly. "Let's make a game of it," Sandor said. "We'll take bets to see how long you can stay alive."

The man grimaced, trying not to show the pain that was ripping him apart from inside out. "Good," he said. "Gives me more time to damn you to hell."

As Sandor's stocky shadow moved away from the

wounded man's face, Liege recognized the DEA agent. It was one of the agents who had been on the cartel's trail for some time now. Liege had seen his file in a batch of dossiers that was sold to the cartels by a contact in the Mexican attorney general's office. Agent Souther. A good man, the kind who kept him on his toes.

Liege clasped Sandor's shoulder and nodded toward the other fallen men on the battlefield. "See to the others," Liege said.

"There's nothing to see," the ex-colonel said. "They're already dead."

Liege clenched Sandor's shoulder with an iron grip that was imperceptible to any of the other men who'd gathered around to watch. But the message was clear. "See to them anyway," Liege stated.

Sandor shrugged and walked away.

The wounded man looked up at him, trying to hold in his ebbing life. Streaks of blood painted his fingers and pooled around his stomach and his thighs.

"I know you," Souther said, squinting through his teary eyes. "You're not Macedonio."

Souther raised a weak hand to shield his eyes from the sun. He recognized the man who towered over him, even with the black hair, even with the wounds dulling his senses. It was the dead-eyed gaze glinting in the sun that gave him away. "Liege," the DEA agent said. "Simon Liege."

"Correct."

"How can you do this to us? You were with SAS. We used to be on the same side."

"There are no sides anymore." Liege said. "There's no good or bad about it. Just winners and losers. We all pull the trigger because we want to. And that's all there is to it."

"Who are you working for?" Souther asked. His voice was growing weak, but his mind was fighting to stay alive.

"I'm with DOA now," Liege said. "I am DOA." He raised the SIG-Sauer P-226 and squeezed the trigger, ending the man's suffering.

As the man's body toppled into the sand, Arturo Sandor came back to Liege's side. "Everyone else is dead and the site's picked clean," he said.

Liege nodded. "It's time to go. But first, let them know who we are."

Sandor picked up the cap that had fallen off Captain Thomas. He held it by the brim and dipped it into the pool of blood on Souther's body. He started writing on the side of the door next to him.

Like blotchy red paint, the streaks of blood spelled out the letters DOA.

They looked like gang colors. Gang warfare.

But the gang was an army.

DOA had declared war.

2

A warm breeze rustled through the chaparral on the edge of the four-thousand-acre ranch, masking the soft footsteps of the man in black.

He stood and waited, listening for the sound of any other predators moving about in the dusk. Nothing. So far he was the only one on the hunt.

Mack Bolan, also known as the Executioner, emerged from the cover of the mesquite and studied the barbed-wire fence with the familiar sign hanging on the post.

A skull and crossbones was emblazoned on the bleached wooden sign with smears of black paint. Beneath the skull were hastily painted words of warning: Trespassers Will Be Met By Lethal Force. It was written in the same style as all of the other signs strung along the past mile of fencing around the ranch.

It was no empty threat. Over the past two years several people had vanished near this stretch of the border. Just three months ago a vigilante rancher from Eagle Pass swore he would stop the influx of traffickers and illegal aliens from Mexico, even if he had to do it single-handedly. He disappeared from the face of the earth. Last seen near the Four Square Ranch.

Six weeks ago a muckraking reporter for a weekly paper filed a story about how a lot of prime Texas ranch land along the Del Rio sector of the U.S. border was being bought out by front men for Mexican and Colombian traffickers. The story paid particular attention to rumors about the Four Square Ranch. It was meant to be the first of a series, but it turned out to be the last story the reporter ever did. His body was found floating in the Rio Grande after serving as fish and crab food for several days. It was almost impossible to tell the cause of death.

No one had ever been charged with the crimes.

But there was no doubt in Bolan's mind who was responsible. Nor was there any doubt in the minds of the few neighboring ranchers who'd refused to sell out to the menacing "buyers" who showed up late at night offering them a fair price for their land. When they didn't sell, instead of threatening them openly, the buyers expressed concern for their safety and promised to return after they had enough time to think it over. Time to get your affairs in order was the most common phrase used by the buyers. Despite the implicit threats, no one was eager to testify in court against the clan of hardcases who'd moved onto the remote ranch within the past year.

It was located near a shallow stretch of water well known to the mules and drug gangs who smuggled illegals and narcotics up from Mexico. For them the gates of the Four Square were always open. There they would find a safe haven before moving on to the next stop on the trafficker's route.

All others would meet lethal force, the man in black thought.

This night he would meet it in kind. Not only were the ranch hands responsible for disappearances of innocent civilians, they were involved in the DOA assault.

He closed the wire cutters around the thick strand of wire and clenched his fist around the handles. With a quick twist he severed the top strand of tightly wound barbed wire. It whipsawed through the air with a harsh metallic song as it uncoiled.

Bolan worked his way toward the ground-level barbed wire, snapping and twisting the cutters until the last wire fell.

He walked through the opening, knowing that he was triggering motion sensors that were planted all across the ranch. He was deliberately feeding information to the enemy. Information they would soon choke on, he thought.

The soldier jogged across the field to the site he'd picked out during an earlier recon, a dip in the grassy field that provided good cover for him and a hazardous approach for anyone else.

Crouching, he unzipped the all-weather gear bag and laid it flat on the ground, revealing an array of weaponry that made him a force to be reckoned with for anyone who came out to deal with the trespasser.

Bolan figured he had about four minutes before someone from the main building responded to the tripped sensors. He used the time to prepare his defenses for the inevitable meeting with the clan, calmly going about the mechanics of death like a craftsman who'd toured many a battlefield.

When he was satisfied with his position, he slid the canvas sheath off the rifle and unfolded the tripod for the bolt-action weapon. He propped his elbow on the ground and aimed the long-range, large caliber rifle toward the killing field. The Accuracy International rifle had a 10-round box magazine and fired .338-caliber armor-piercing rounds.

The Executioner's latest tour had begun.

He settled in and listened for the sound of their approach.

Within two minutes the loud angry whine of a tortured engine shattered the evening silence. Moments later it was joined by another, better tuned vehicle.

A Ford Explorer bounced over the farthest ridge, going airborne for several seconds before coming down hard and kicking up a cloud of dust. It was heading straight for him from a distance of two hundred yards.

It was the same Ford Explorer that had been captured on surveillance footage of the Border Patrol massacre. That vehicle and a few others were tracked to the ranch by the NSA monitoring team on-site for the handoff of Jorge Macedonio.

The striking force had split up after wiping out the American drug warriors. Some of them headed straight back into Mexico. Others had traveled along the Rio Grande in a roundabout way before making their way back to the ranch.

It was standard operating procedure for the cartels. They had fleets of vehicles on both sides of the border that could move illegal aliens or contraband at high speed. They also had battle wagons like the thing that appeared right behind the Explorer.

The battered old farm truck with worn-out shocks clanked and clattered downhill, a heap of groaning metal that nearly spilled the occupants in the flatbed. There were a half dozen hardmen back there with, presumably, a truckload of automatic weapons.

The cavalry was coming en masse, expecting easy prey.

A fatal assumption.

The Executioner tracked the rifle's scope across the Explorer's windshield, scanning the occupants inside.

Two men in the front.

Three shooters in the back.

It was a fair-sized welcoming committee and as their images grew larger through the scope, he saw that they had a hell of a welcome in mind.

The man in the passenger seat was literally riding shotgun, jabbing the barrel of a drum magazine "street sweeper" out the window. His beefy left hand gripped the carry handle of the USAS-12 shotgun so he could get a better field of fire.

Bolan recognized the special operations piece. It was a ten-pound package, made a little bit heavier by the 28-round drum that was packed with 12-gauge man-shredders. It had a semiautomatic or full-automatic switch, and it could throw down a lot of suppressing fire in an extremely short time.

In the right hands a weapon like that could make Bolan disappear, just like the others who'd vanished on the ranch. But was it in the right hands? he wondered as the shotgunner poked his head out the window for a clearer look at the killing field. The sudden rush of wind blew off his floppy hat, revealing an unkempt halo of bushy hair.

A latter-day Viking, Bolan thought. He was on a wild ride, a primordial wild hunt, whooping and yelling as the thrill of the chase drowned every trace of civilized man within him and washed it away in blood frenzy. The man was like a hunter following the hounds to his treed prey.

The driver gunned the Explorer straight for Bolan, almost as if he could see him. Bolan told himself it was just his mind playing tricks on him. After all, he was between the hunting party and the gap in the fence.

There was no way they could see him.

And then the shotgun roared, spitting fiery blasts from the revolving drum magazine. The ground erupted in front of Bolan. Volcanic thuds exploded all around him as the high-impact rounds spit out from the smoking barrel of the Daewoo USAS-12 shotgun. He had it on full-automatic, digging up furrows of ground all around him.

Gunfire scythed the air overhead as the men in the pickup joined in, burning clip after clip in his direction.

They had better surveillance than he'd expected, Bolan thought. Maybe some video relays spiked into the hills that turned this part of the range into a private broadcast back at the main house. Or maybe they were just reconning by fire, figuring if they shot enough lead they were bound to hit something.

Either way, it was time.

He exhaled and pulled the trigger. The heavy-caliber round blew off the top of the Explorer's windshield and sent a shower of glass and metal shards raining into the air. But the driver kept coming, heading full speed toward Bolan—full speed toward two more .338-caliber slugs.

The Accuracy International rounds disintegrated the bony shield of the driver's forehead and sprayed the wet tissue of his brain onto the gunmen in the back seat, sharing his last thoughts with them.

The steering wheel spun out of control. The Explorer lurched sideways, then tumbled end over end, scrambling the battered bodies inside before coming to a stop upside down, wheels spinning, smoke pouring from the hood.

The bushy-haired shotgunner erupted from the window and staggered onto the grassy battlefield in a daze, waving the street sweeper like a scepter.

Bolan didn't wait to see if the man had anything left in the 28-round shotgun. He nailed him with an armor-piercing round that cored through his head and dropped him.

He triggered two more slugs into the Explorer's gas tank, turning it into an instant crematorium for the gunners in the back seat.

That left the pickup. Its blunt nose careened off the back of the burning SUV, riding through sheets of flame before it went into an uncontrolled spin. The driver of the ancient farm truck stomped on the brakes and brought it to a tilting stop. It teetered on edge and was about to land upright. But then the ground gave out beneath the thick heavy wheels and it flipped over on its side, shedding rusted fenders like fossils.

A cursing cluster of human cargo tumbled out in a tangle of limbs and weaponry. Two DOA gunners did unintentional back flips and fell behind the truck. The other four men were caught in a web of splinters as the side-rail slats broke apart on impact. They staggered to their feet, shrugging off the gashes from the needle-sharp pieces of wood.

The floor of the flatbed loomed behind them, making it

look like a lineup at the police station. But Bolan wasn't asking any questions.

He tracked the Beretta 93-R from right to left and squeezed off 3-round bursts that dropped the gunners in a deadly cadence. A few of the rounds thwacked into the wood behind them, but the others found their target.

Bolan took a head count on the farm team.

Four bullet-riddled bodies lay on the ground.

One driver was still in the flame-scorched cab.

That left two men unaccounted for. Two men who were damaged from the crash or seeking shelter behind the overturned truck.

Instead of playing a deadly game of hide-and-seek, the Executioner put down the Beretta and scooped up the pistol-shaped grenade launcher beside his carryall. Four pounds of awesome firepower that was as elegant as it was lethal. And the curved retracted stock made it compact enough to tuck into a deep khaki pocket for operations where discretion was a factor.

The Executioner pulled back on the foot-long stock of the Heckler & Koch M-69 40 mm launcher until it was fully extended. Then he jammed the butt of the stock against his shoulder and tugged back on the trigger, absorbing the shock of the high explosive grenade round catapulting from the thick metal tube.

It went off like a cannon shot, ripping through the flatbed floor and showering explosives onto the sheltered DOA troopers.

Bolan rolled to his left and thumped another 40 mm grenade into the smoking debris just to make sure there were no surprises waiting for him on the other side. There were a dozen more 40 mm rounds in the pouches on his web belt, containing smoke, CS, flares and fléchettes but the back of the truck and the people behind it had been transformed into smoking ruins.

He put down the grenade launcher, threw a fresh magazine into the Beretta, then circled to check on the out of luck truckers.

Two more dead.

Only the driver was alive. Half alive, anyway. His face had been seared by the sheets of flame from the Ford Explorer that jumped across the windows as the two vehicles collided. It had scorched the windshield and the man behind the wheel. The roof of the cab had also crumpled inward like a metal spear and left a deep puncture wound on his temple. The back window had exploded into a thousand tiny crystals of glass that coated his back like blood-soaked sequins.

Bolan reached inside and grabbed the back of the man's collar, twisted it to get a firm handhold, then tugged him into the open.

The man flopped on the ground with strips of burned skin peeling off his face and neck like one of the living dead. Half of his face was baked a corpse-colored black. Blood covered his throat and breastbone.

"Can you talk?" Bolan asked.

"Yes," he grunted through his raw lips. "But I'm hurt."

"Yeah," Bolan said, glancing at the corpses scattered on the ground. "Compared to the rest of your pals, you just won the lottery. Providing you can answer some questions, you might go on living. You want that?"

The man looked up into the eyes of the Executioner and saw a hard-faced man with no room for pity.

"Yes," he said.

"Good. How many more in the house?" Bolan asked.

"No one."

"You all came out here for the party?"

"That's right."

"I'd like to believe you," Bolan said. He nodded toward the horizon where another vehicle was traveling along the fence line. Lights out. Going *away* from the firefight. It came to a sudden stop. The dome light flashed briefly as the occupant got out of the car and hurried to the fence. Probably a section of fence that was rigged to act as a gate if someone knew where to look, Bolan thought. He glanced back down at the damaged man. "But my senses tell me otherwise."

The man was about to protest, but then his mouth froze, his eyes closed, and he was gone. No more lies would pass from his lips.

Bolan was walking away when he heard a muffled mechanical voice coming from the dead driver.

"Golden?"

The Executioner crouched over the body. A burst of static came from the fallen man's front pocket and the voice sounded again, as if he were a ventriloquist's dummy. "Golden. Come in." Even through the hiss, the man's desperation was obvious.

Bolan reached into the driver's pocket and pulled out a boxy little two-way radio. "Yeah," Bolan said into the transceiver, doing his best to impersonate the man he'd only heard briefly. The voice of a dying man at that. "Go ahead."

"Who is this?"

"You're the one who called. Who do you think it is?"

"Don't fuck with me!"

"I haven't really started yet," Bolan said.

"Let me talk to someone else."

The Executioner surveyed the carnage around him. "You know how to reach the dead?" he asked.

"What?"

"They're all dead," Bolan said. "Now you can join the rest of your crew in eternal rest or you can cooperate with us—"

The line went dead and the last man left alive on the Four

Square Ranch drove off through the makeshift gate, heading toward the Rio Grande and his masters across the border.

Bolan tossed the two-way radio onto the ground, then headed back to the spot where he first dug in. He picked up the secure encrypted satellite phone and called Hal Brognola, director of the Sensitive Operations Group. "There's only one left," Bolan said, "and he's on the run."

"Good," the head Fed responded. "I'll put the Never Say Anything crew on it, see where he leads us." Like several other covert agencies currently being fielded by Brognola, the NSA was tasked with locating the DOA leader and any of the cartel backers who spawned him. They'd been on alert, waiting for the Executioner to flush them out.

"What about the rest of them?" Brognola asked.

"Send in the black flight crew to bag 'em, box 'em and bury 'em," Bolan said. "I'll meet them up at the main house and see what I can find."

"The birds are on their way," Brognola told him. "Meanwhile keep your suitcase packed. We're taking off as soon as you get back here."

"Where to?"

"I'll tell you on the plane."

Thirty minutes later a detachment of unmarked helicopters from Fort Bliss landed on the Four Square Ranch. They came in low and silent and carried a well-trained force of special ops troops.

The counterinsurgency and drug war commandos spread out across the ranch, removing the remains of the DOA soldiers. They also carted up the intelligence treasure trove that Bolan had found inside the main house. Computers, phones, weapons. Anything that could add another footprint to the trail of DOA.

By the time they were done, the ranch was eerily silent and empty. There was no trace of the hardmen who had literally spent their lives there. There would be nothing about them in the paper or on the news.

Traffickers who crossed the border expecting to find a safe haven would instead find themselves entering a danger zone. The message was unmistakable. Anyone who set foot on the ranch from here on in might come down with lead poisoning.

3

The Gates Learjet had a lot of stand-up headroom, which suited Hal Brognola just fine as he paced back and forth in the plush airborne office that was flying him and Bolan down to Belize.

There were plenty of military craft available at Fort Bliss but in light of the current war footing with DOA, there was no need to advertise the fact that some serious individuals were onboard.

Though it looked like a civil aircraft, the jet that streaked across the Gulf of Mexico had advanced communications and evasion components that didn't come with the typical Lear model.

Brognola was in another one of his crisis modes. What else was new, Bolan thought. Considering the number of high-level snafus that landed on his desk, the head Fed was constantly putting out fires. But this one was out of the ordinary, even for Brognola. This one threatened to burn out of control and lay waste to the country if they didn't throw everything they had on it.

Which was why Bolan was flying over the Gulf at four o'clock in the morning, looking out the window at the fathomless dark. The jet was flying a route that kept them far away from Mexican airspace, mainly because of the disturbing implications of the Del Rio massacre.

The Mexican government had always had been an uncertain ally in the drug war, particularly since so many generals, attorneys general and politicians were in the pockets of the cartels. In recent years one-third of the Federal Judicial Police force had been fired or jailed for crimes ranging from theft and smuggling to murder for hire. And those were only the ones foolish enough to get caught.

It was just as well known that for the right price, units of the Mexican military would provide escort services to the traffickers or rent out airstrips to them. The only real danger to traffickers occurred when they fell out of favor with their police or military sponsors. That usually meant the police had switched allegiance and were now working for a different cartel. Eventually, the police would swoop in on their former employers, kill those who might expose them and extort ransoms from the ones they let go. While there were some outstanding members in the Mexican antidrug units who Brognola could trust, they were rapidly becoming an endangered species.

The situation with Mexico was uppermost in Brognola's thoughts as he continued his restless prowl up and down the cabin while Bolan scanned the stack of dossiers spread out on the desk.

"I still can't believe he's in the dark on this," Brognola said, fuming over his latest discussion with Emilio Darien, his counterpart in the upper ranks of Mexican intelligence. Darien was a military adviser to the new president who oversaw millions of dollars of antidrug money provided by the U.S. A covert audit by the NSA's crypto cops tracked most of those funds to luxury villas and cars owned by Darien and his underlings. It helped the drug warriors relax from the strain of pretending to catch the real criminals.

Brognola was used to such corruption. It was standard operating procedure in most of the countries officially certified by the U.S. as zealous allies in the war against drugs. But there usually was some kind of quid pro quo. The government receiving U.S. aid was supposed to maintain the illusion that they were committed to the same cause. And when they were pressed, the government was supposed to provide real intelligence.

It just wasn't happening in this case. Darien had assured Brognola that Mexican authorities had absolutely no knowledge of any such force as DOA, had noticed nothing unusual on their side of the border, and had no idea how the terrorist group acquired official army and police uniforms. He also had no idea of the whereabouts of Jorge Macedonio and doubted he was even in the country. "But he promised to look into it for us," Brognola said. "I'd be happy if he just stopped looking the other way, for Christ's sake."

"That's not going to happen, Hal," Bolan said. "Not until we force him into a corner. We're a long way from that point."

Brognola sighed. "You're right, Striker. I'm just getting it off my chest. No one in Washington likes to hear this kind of talk."

"Vent away, guy," Bolan said. "I'll listen. But you're preaching to the choir. I hate it just as much as you do. Just part of the playing field."

Brognola nodded. "Yeah. You're right, you're right." His voice drifted off. Then he went over to the coffee service in the corner and grabbed a carafe of coffee to refresh his bottomless mug.

Bolan glanced at the man charged with fielding one of the largest covert task forces in his entire career. He looked tired but not beaten. Somehow he would summon up the energy to get through this. And Bolan would help him every step of the way. That was the deal forged between them so long ago. Each would take care of his own end. Brognola would handle the administrative side of things and cover Bolan's back while Bolan took care of the executive action.

Sometimes it was difficult to tell which was the harder war to fight. The planning or the execution. Bolan didn't envy Brognola one bit. As the President's go-to guy for covert operations, Brognola had his assets working around the clock in the cocaine countries that were linked to the emerging DOA threat. So far that included Mexico, Colombia, Peru and Belize. All part of a growing list.

The big Fed was also sending in several U.S. Special Forces units to link up with their contacts in the Belize Defense Force. Fortunately, they had a strong working relationship with the Belizeans. When the British left their former colony to its own devices, the BDF quickly cemented relationships with the U.S. They routinely participated in joint training missions throughout Belize and the Caribbean. Because of those training exercises many Special Forces teams were familiar with the cayes and coastlines of Belize as well as the forests.

Tucked beneath the southeast corner of Mexico's Yucatán Peninsula, the tiny Central American country was a stauncher ally in the drug war than Mexico would ever be. The government of Belize had no choice in the matter, since it was constantly under assault from the cartels. As the perfect transshipment point for cocaine and heroin from Colombia and Peru, it was being groomed to become the next Panama.

The cartels planned on creating a Belizean haven for offshore banks and the fugitives who laundered their money through them. It would be a country controlled by an alliance of cartels. Other cabals had tried to take over Belize in the past, but this was the first time they fielded an army to help them do it. An army that could cross borders and strike its enemies at will.

That was the plan, anyway. It was Bolan's job to derail it.

He sifted through the dossiers that Brognola had assembled from the various intelligence services, particularly the NSA, CIA and DEA. Knowing that his life could depend upon his ability to recall the information or recognize a face at a moment's notice, Bolan went through each file several times in order to commit them to memory.

Even though he was fresh off the mission at Four Square, Bolan was nowhere as tired as Brognola. Back at Fort Bliss he grabbed an hour's worth of sleep, then woke himself up with a bracing shower before boarding the jet and getting on with the business at hand.

The Executioner held a blowup of the man believed to be the head of DOA, the stand-in for Macedonio who orchestrated the slaughter on the border. The photo was taken from NSA footage that had been digitized, enhanced and converted into thermal face prints and morphed into several alternative profiles of the subject. Bolan knew the drill. Everything that could possibly be done to a graphic image had been done to this one, probably even photo brushing it to remove pimples, he thought. Then it was fed into the massive data banks at Fort Meade, Maryland, and circulated at the speed of satellite through every other computer linked to the law-enforcement community.

The alert had gone out and it had been answered in less than twenty-four hours, a testament to the efficiency of the covert computer corps. Though Bolan was an action man, he gave them their due. More and more it was the desktop commandos who zeroed in on the targets he went after. Of course it helped matters that the current target was a known commodity in the covert community. Just about every intelligence service in the world had considerable files on him. At one time or another he had worked for them or against them.

"Simon Liege," Bolan said out loud, looking at the face of the rogue soldier with the glassy right eye, a dead zone picked up by the NSA's thermal scan. It was listed as one of his identifying marks in the capsule summary at the bottom of the photograph. The summary also identified him as a former trooper with the British SAS and SBS who retired from the service and went into private security work.

Liege often did assignments for his old bosses in the SAS when they needed a cutout to insure their deniability. His most frequent task for them was recruiting, outfitting and leading mercenaries on British-backed missions. There was a brief scandal when he worked on the wrong side of an attempted coup in the Seychelles, and there were rumors of his involvement in other shady affairs. But he was still a member in good standing in the famous SAS Good Old Boy Network. They even brought him back into the fold for an extended tour in Belize, where he helped train the BDF when the British still had a stake in their former colony.

Bolan looked through some of the other photos in the manila-jacketed folder. Each showed a different side of the mercenary. There was the family man photo that showed him with a young former wife and two children in front of their London home. She was beautiful and sad looking at the same time, as if she knew the man beside her was a temporary guest in her life.

There was also a clandestine shot of him taken in Gibraltar where he had a vacation home that was often frequented by out of work mercs. And there was even a mug shot of him during his Seychelles adventure when he was briefly jailed for his role in the coup.

All water under the bridge, Bolan thought. Typical resume of a covert warrior.

But when did the man switch sides?

Bolan found the answer in a tersely written report behind the photos. It all started when Liege took a covert assignment for the Colombian government and led an elite force of mercs against a guerrilla-linked cartel.

Liege's people assassinated the leadership and most of the guerrillas working for them. It was a success all around—until word got out that instead of working on behalf of the Colombia government, Liege was actually working for a competing cartel that wanted to remove the competition.

From then on, Liege offered his services to other cartels. Recruiting bodyguards, training cartel gunmen, fending off government drug units and special forces troops. His clients were a loosely organized group of cartels from Peru and Colombia up through Mexico, where his main sponsor was Jorge Macedonio. Liege's main base of operations was believed to the south of Mexico and in Belize, his old stomping grounds.

Simon Liege was an ambitious man.

Instead of merely defending the cartels, Liege had taken it to the next step. He'd gone on the offensive. His current specialty was seeking vengeance on the U.S. government, the ultimate enemy behind the secret war against the cartels. Until now it had been a one-sided war.

But Liege had made it clear he was ready to cross any border to seek out the enemy. The name he chose for his army was obviously a grotesque perversion of the DEA, the longtime nemesis of the cartels. DOA. Dead on arrival.

That could work both ways, Bolan thought as he probed through the other dossiers, learning more about Liege's background and associates. Finally he stacked the last dossier on top of the pile. "That's it," Bolan said.

"Not quite," Brognola said, stirring from the white leather couch on the other side of the cabin. He reached into his worn leather briefcase and took out a slim file. "This came in while you were scoping out the ranch. Its existence is known to a very few. We've got to keep it that way, Striker."

"What's so special about it?" Bolan asked.

Brognola walked over to the desktop and dropped the file onto its surface with a loud whack. "It's the nail in the coffin for DOA," he said, tapping his finger on top of the file.

The head Fed rested his hand on top of the other stack of files. "As you probably gathered from the rest of the intel, the DOA scenario we put together is based on a lot of variables. Except for the surveillance footage, it relies on a fair amount of conjecture and analysis of Liege's associations with cartel figures. It's a pretty solid piece of work, but it's got some guesswork."

"It had some gaps," Bolan agreed. "But it was a start."

"Let's hope this is the finish," Brognola said. "Take a look."

The soldier flipped open the folder. At first glance he saw a photograph of three mercenaries in jungle camouflage. The hard faces with the mile-long stares looked familiar, but soldiers in the jungle always had that look about them.

"We've got confirmation about Liege's activities from an inside source," Brognola said.

"How reliable?"

"You be the judge," Brognola said. He tapped the photograph, zeroing in on the man in the middle. "Take a closer look at that guy."

The soldier brought the photograph closer and recognized the face from his past. "Jesus Christ," he said.

"Not quite," Brognola said. "Even though we could use a miracle."

"Carvaggio."

Nicholas Carvaggio. Former Mob soldier. Former Special Forces op. Former fugitive from the Justice Department.

The last time Bolan had seen him had been during the Judas Kill operation.

There were a few more lines added to the face, Bolan thought, but there was no mistaking him. Considering the man's explosive background, his photograph almost seemed innocuous. There was nothing intrinsically frightening about the hit man. His dark hair was cut short and combed back in an old-fashioned style, almost like a matinee idol. It was the face of a man who knew how to make his way in life. The only sinister aspect was in the eyes. Eyes that peered out as if they were measuring you for a coffin.

Nicholas Carvaggio. The Executioner had never expected to see him again, let alone encounter him in an operation like this. In a way Bolan was surprised the man was still alive. He was the kind of guy who lived on the edge and was always in danger of falling off.

Carvaggio had once been a major underworld figure who worked for an offshoot of the Sienna crime family in New York City. It was known as the Garrison, an unstoppable street mob composed of Mafia soldiers—real-life soldiers who'd gone into the service and gotten their lethal training. Then they brought their skills back to the war zones of Manhattan.

Carvaggio worked for the Garrison for years. And then one day he started to work against them. He had absolutely no choice in the matter. He was given an assignment to carry out a hit on a female witness in a Mafia trial. She was an innocent witness and therefore untouchable in Carvaggio's eyes. Anyone in the underworld was fair game, but he drew the line at wasting civilians, especially a woman. That put him on the firing line with the Garrison. Its members went after him with everything they had.

And they lost.

Carvaggio joined forces with the only group that could save him. The Justice Department wanted the Garrison more than they wanted a single gunner like Carvaggio. Brognola tasked Bolan with bringing him in. The two of them fought side by side in their private war against the Garrison.

After the Mob war was over, Carvaggio was allowed to go on his way. All of his sins were forgiven provided he stayed on the straight and narrow. But at the moment, he seemed pretty far afield.

"I see you remember him," Brognola said.

"Hard guy to forget," Bolan said. "Straight shooter. Knows what he's about. Doesn't play around. Always goes in for the kill."

Brognola smiled. "Yeah. Could almost be your twin."

Bolan dropped the photograph on the desk. "He with DOA?"

"Yeah. That picture was taken right after Liege's anti-cartel operation in Colombia. It made for some good propaganda. The usual noble mercenary stuff. It appeared in the Bogotá newspapers back when everyone thought the mercs were white knights. Even appeared in some of our own news rags. Headlines said it was another great victory in the drug war. No one had a clue it was only a victory for Simon Liege."

"What was Carvaggio's role?" Bolan asked. He liked the ex-Garrison gunman a great deal. The Executioner had stood side by side with him and a couple of times had even placed his life in Carvaggio's hands. But if the hit man had strayed, he would have to be treated just like the rest of the enemy. With extreme prejudice. "How'd he get mixed up with DOA?"

"Recruited by an outfit in Gibraltar that's connected to Liege. At the time it was all completely up and up. Carvaggio signed on expecting to take out some cartel killers in Colombia. The kind of merc work sanctioned by our British friends. He didn't find out what Liege was really about until the Del Rio hit went down."

"Was Carvaggio involved in that?" Bolan asked.

Brognola shook his head. "No, just the Colombia strike and a few other operations against cartels. No crime in that. But he contacted us after he learned about the border massacre."

"Where is he now?"

"Hard to say," Brognola replied. "Liege moves his people around a lot. He maintains safehouses and training camps for his mercs up and down Central America. Carvaggio managed to steal enough time to contact our embassy in Belize. He dropped enough names on them to get his information passed up through channels until it got on my desk. It was cryptic, but if I read him right, Carvaggio plans on staying with DOA until he can take out Liege himself. Or point you in the right direction."

"It's a dangerous game," Bolan said. "But he's the right guy to play it."

"He helped us once. We'll see if he's still got it in him. But first, let's get you situated on why we're *both* flying down to Belize. I'm meeting with some of the powers that be. You'll be meeting with someone who definitely *won't* want to meet with you. He's one of the guys who took part in the Del Rio hit."

Bolan nodded, then threw Carvaggio's dossier on top of the other files. He listened to the big Fed's briefing about a key member of DOA who'd been tracked to Belize. When the briefing was over, he dropped back in the comfortable seat, closed his eyes and drifted off until he was awakened by one of the flight crew.

The air steward was obviously a military man despite the commercial airline uniform he wore. "We'll be landing shortly," he said to the soldier. "Is there anything you need?"

Yeah, Bolan thought. A return to yesteryear. The good old days when a steward was a stewardess and was worth waking up for. But all he said was, "I could use a cup of coffee."

The steward looked over at Brognola, who was stretched out on the couch, with an empty carafe on the table beside him. "Sorry," he said. "It's all gone. Unless you want us to make some more?"

"Thanks anyway," Bolan said. "I'll survive."

Twenty minutes later they landed at Belize City where Bolan disembarked as an American businessman named Michael Belasko. Brognola stayed onboard for the second leg of the journey to Belmopan, the new capital of Belize, deep in the interior. The old one kept getting washed out from the hurricanes that pounded the coastline.

Bolan's itinerary was set for him. Eventually, he was supposed to stay at an Agency-run villa north of Belize, but first he had a private charter waiting to take him out to Emerald Caye, a secluded island preserve that catered to an exclusive clientele.

There were a few pricey resorts on the island, some private homes and an unpaved airstrip that had most recently flown in a high-ranking officer of the DOA.

The man's name was Arturo Sandor. Before he returned to civilian life he'd served in several branches of the military, most recently as a colonel in the Mexican army.

Bolan stepped out of the airport terminal into the hot and humid steam bath that was Belize on a cool day.

He walked down the street to the nearest hotel, had a cup of coffee and grabbed one of the local papers. Then he called a cab to take him down to a Hattieville marina where a sportfishing boat awaited him.

It was supposed to be fully stocked with everything he needed. Plenty of fishing gear, bait and enough covert weaponry to troll through Emerald Caye.

4

Belize was a tropical paradise, Bolan thought.

When it wasn't raining. Since the rainy season lasted for three-quarters of the year, that wasn't too often. Brief and sudden storms came out of nowhere and drenched everything in the country. The downpours faded just as suddenly as they sprang up, quickly replaced by a bright unforgiving sun and a blanket of humidity.

Thanks to the rainfall, almost eighty percent of the country was considered to be rain forest. At the moment Bolan was soaking wet, a sodden soldier in a hot climate, knowing that it would take his body a good day or two before he began to acclimate to the temperature.

But time was a luxury he didn't have, so he continued walking at a fast clip toward the private marina just south of Hattieville. His socks squished with every step, and the back of his white cotton shirt stuck to his shoulders. The storm had stopped but its gifts stayed with him.

The soldier had followed his usual precautions and climbed out of the taxi from Belize City a good mile away from his actual destination. Shortly after he started walking along the winding coastal road, the rain dropped from the sky like a liquid bombardment. Dim curtains of rain washed out most of the visibility.

He'd been forced to seek shelter for the duration, not because of the weather, but because of the local Belizean drivers who weren't about to change their Indianapolis 500 speeding tactics due to a little rain. To avoid a future as roadkill, Bolan waited out the storm on the edge of a mud-lined gully between the road and a cluster of mangroves. He sat with his waterproof windbreaker draped over his head while keeping an eye out for snakes and other creatures washed out by the storm. Welcome to Belize, he thought.

The storm ceased after a relatively short twenty minutes and the sun was out, baking the asphalt beneath his feet. He felt almost dehydrated. It was too damned hot for this early in the morning, he told himself. But then he'd been in worse weather than this and in a hell of a lot of worse situations. At least no one was shooting at him. Not yet anyway.

Bolan did his best to ignore the heat as he continued walking toward his rendezvous with a special agent from the U.S. Customs Service who was slated to take him into battle.

Fifteen minutes later Bolan's footsteps rumbled down the long wooden dock of a private marina. He walked straight into a breeze that hissed across the diamond-capped sea and washed away the humid air.

A sleek single hull Chris-Craft Stinger waited at the end of the dock. An even sleeker captain sat behind the wheel in the cockpit listening to a Jimmy Buffett tune.

She spun to face him, looking him up and down from her shaded perch beneath the white canvas canopy.

"Don't look so shocked," she said, reaching behind her to turn down the radio. "I can handle myself if that's what you're wondering."

He was wondering a lot of things but all he said was, "I'm sure you're more than qualified." He realized he hadn't totally covered up his surprise. He'd expected to meet an old salt named Sandy Rowan. "Otherwise you wouldn't be here. Right?"

"Right," she said, stepping out into the sunlight and re-vealing more of her lithe figure. Long tan legs in cut off shorts, midriff-baring white top that was snug around her breasts, reddish-blond hair that glittered like a crimson lure in the sun.

Not exactly his idea of a seagoing commando.

"You must be Belasko," she said.

Bolan nodded. "And you must be Captain Rowan."

"Captain of the ship and captain of my fate," she said. "So don't treat me different from anyone else you worked with. I chose this line of work, and I've been at it for fifteen years now and haven't been killed once."

He liked her easygoing manner. Probably one of the things that kept her alive in such a dangerous profession. "I think we'll get along fine," Bolan said.

"Then come aboard."

The soldier clambered down a few rungs on the dock ladder, then jumped into the back of the thirty-nine footer. He tossed his small pack onto the seat.

"You're traveling light," she commented.

"A change of clothes and a couple changes of identity," Bolan said. "I understood arrangements were being made for the other stuff."

She slid her hand along a side compartment and popped the latch. The door opened outward, revealing several kit bags, packs and weapons cases. "Everything you asked for is right here," she said. "Plus a few extras I thought we might need when we get out there."

"How long will it take?"

"Your typical fast boat will make it to Emerald Caye in two hours," she said, as she slipped off the last remaining rope that tethered them to the dock.

Bolan surveyed the modified Chris-Craft. "And this one?"

"An hour and a half," she said. "If the sea's not too rough." She climbed behind the wheel and started the engines, which churned the water with a low guttural sound as she eased the boat into the open water.

"Here," she said, tossing him a life vest. "Sit back and enjoy it."

She gave it full throttle.

The sudden surge of power boosted the seaborne rocket out of the cove in seconds, leaving a frothing wake behind it. The needle-shaped bow that gave the Stinger its name shot out of the water while the twin engines roared at 4200 rpm. Sea spray splashed into the boat from both sides, dipping under the windblown canopy as the customs drug buster bucked across the water, firmly planting Bolan in the white bucket seat.

The Stinger was part of a fleet used by U.S. Customs to catch the souped-up cigarette boats used by traffickers who had the money to burn. The rakish craft had been repainted a misty cerulean blue instead of the warlike red-and-white paint it wore in its old incarnation. The idea was to make it look like a kinder, gentler speedboat. A boat that wouldn't seem out of place with the other pleasure boats that flocked to Emerald Caye.

But it still had most of the covert conveniences of the official customs boats, including state-of-the-art communications gear, transponders, radar units, lights and loudspeakers. And it could still move.

Sandy Rowan proved that by bringing them to Emerald Caye just under the hour and a half mark.

Like many of the larger keys off the Belizean coast, it was undergoing a lot of development, evidenced by the resorts and villas sprouting up on the western side of the island.

Yachts, cabin cruisers and tour boats trolled up and down the coast, clustering in the sheltered bays where the upscale resorts and rental properties were located.

The misty blue Chris-Craft nosed into Emerald Caye well

before noon and began a tour of the shoreline, mingling with the other pleasure craft that lazily prowled offshore.

"There it is, Belasko."

Bolan looked to the right where the captain was pointing. A six-story hotel rose out of tall palms and mangroves that flanked it on both sides. Set back from the shore, it looked like a hybrid of a Mayan pyramid and a Holiday Inn. Sandstone terraces trimmed with cedarwood frames looked down on an L-shaped pool below. The pool was sealed off from the outside world by elegant wrought-iron fencing.

It catered to the kind of guest who could afford to spend a small fortune for a one-night stay. Guests like Arturo Sandor. He and his retinue had taken over the top two floors of the hotel and populated it with a choice selection of playmates who were even more expensive than the rooms.

"What do you think?" Bolan asked. "Pretty nice digs for a guy with a colonel's salary."

"He probably invested wisely," she said. "Built himself a nice little nest egg."

"Too bad he won't be around to spend it."

"Maybe he knows that already," she said. "Maybe that's why he's in a hurry to spend it while he can."

Bolan shook his head. "No. This one's totally in the dark. Thinks he'll live forever now that he's got DOA behind him."

The colonel was totally unaware that his movements had been tracked by the NSA and a half dozen other agencies ever since he took part in the DOA's cross-border assault in Del Rio. Nor did he have any idea that his identity was even known to the opposition.

It was all fun and games for the ex-army gunman who was rewarding his inner circle for a campaign well fought.

The Executioner scanned the hotel with a pair of binoculars, tracking across the front of the palatial estate floor by floor. He paid special attention to the forests that almost brushed against the sides of the latter-day pyramid, their branches rising almost all the way up to the third floor.

Bolan studied the complex as if it were a mountain to be scaled and saw plenty of potential handholds. Lots of corners and ledges on the stepping-stone terraces that tapered off near the top. It looked easy enough to get up, he thought, if he took his time. But it would be a lot harder going down in a hurry. Especially if the colonel's men were around to take potshots at him.

There were plenty of people around. Some of them were civilians, some were hardmen. It could get messy if they didn't know who was who.

"We'll have to do it tonight," Bolan said.

"It's your call," she replied. "I'll be ready when you are."

For the next couple of hours they drifted offshore, taking turns spying on the hotel grounds and identifying the colonel's men as they lounged around the pool, totally focused on the professional women splashing in the water.

Bolan and Rowan also took turns grabbing sleep. They had to be good to go when the time came.

IT WAS EARLY EVENING. The sun was still out, but the oppressive midday heat was gone, washed away by the gentle Caribbean wind that swept across the bay.

Almost like being on a vacation, Bolan thought. If vacations could be measured in hours. That was the amount of time left before they launched the strike.

From Bolan's point of view beneath the canopy of the observation post floating in the middle of Emerald Caye, the hotel facade looked like a fortress. And the recessed terraces looked like bunkers. Adding to the militant appearance was a blue Belizean flag with its white coat of arms fluttering from a rooftop pole.

But it was more facade than fort. He knew it well thanks

to the afternoon they'd spent in the bay with a hundred other boats in the changing fleet of pleasure crafts.

Now and then they'd taken the Stinger on a high-speed run, just to shake off their surveillance fatigue and catch some wind in their faces. But they always returned to the bay and dropped anchor once again to study their prey.

Like watching creatures in the wild, Bolan thought, as he thumbed the magnification wheel on the binoculars and zoomed in on the top-floor terrace. No, Bolan thought, when the two figures came into view. It was more like a spectator sport.

The colonel was back in action.

He was cavorting with the catch of the day, an artificially endowed party girl who'd done a hundred laps in the pool and a hundred more on the terrace.

She looked like a prize at a carnival, a toy doll painted with too many conflicting colors. Her hair was mostly blond, and her skin had the orange hue that came only from a chemical tan.

An impossible girl to ignore, Bolan thought. Physically impossible. Her pneumatic breasts had been built by an extremely talented or demented surgeon. Not only were they in danger of slipping from her bikini top, which was little more than a pair of bright neon eye patches connected by a thin string, but they threatened to topple her over the balcony.

The colonel stood behind her, embracing her briefly, before untying the knot of the bikini top and waving it like a captured flag.

The sculpted breasts beamed from the balcony in all of their silicone glory.

"Don't tell me," said the soft voice next to him. "Let me guess. She's back again."

The soldier glanced at the Stinger pilot, sitting in the cockpit chair to his right, resting her legs on a cooler full of bottled water and iced coffee. She lifted her sunglasses and peered out at him. "Well?"

"How can you tell?" he asked.

"I majored in anthropology before switching to criminal justice," she said. "We studied a lot of mating rituals, primarily signals given off by the male. You know, subtle things like gasping, groaning and drooling."

"I was just admiring the architecture," Bolan said. "Identifying the friendlies from the hostiles."

Rowan reached for the binoculars and quickly zeroed in on the upper floor. "I see what you mean," she said. "This one looks very friendly. And that kind of *architecture* defies the laws of gravity. I'd like to see her in five years."

"So would I," Bolan said.

She raised her eyebrows. "I didn't think you stuck around long enough to see the same girl twice."

"Right," Bolan said, as he took back the binoculars. "Was that in your briefing packet?"

"No," she stated. "Just an educated guess. It's the same for everybody in this business, isn't it? You don't form too many lasting attachments. You either move on, or they do. One way or another."

The sense of loss in her voice was unmistakable. Obviously, there was someone she'd been extremely close to on one of her previous stints with the Agency, DEA or Customs Service. Someone who had probably moved permanently beyond her reach. It was an occupational hazard.

He knew what it felt like to lose someone that close, someone he expected to see for the rest of his life but had to go on living it without. Friends, family, lovers. A shifting gallery of faces suddenly swam through his thoughts. Faces of people who were still alive in his dreams, but had to go back to their graves when he woke. Voices he'd never hear again.

They were all victims of his everlasting war.

Victims who were too close to Bolan for their own good.

The Executioner discreetly studied Rowan. Early thirties and all natural, she was more beautiful than the woman on the balcony could ever hope to be. Lithe and lean, smart. Piercing eyes that didn't let you off the hook. She had that outdoors look about her that appealed to Bolan, a woman who definitely led an unsheltered life.

It was impossible not to recognize the magnetism between them, the attractions as well as the dangers. Two people thrown together in a high-risk mission like this could throw off a lot of sparks. But now wasn't the time, Bolan thought. To act upon that attraction might add a couple more casualties to the war.

If and when they got through this, however...

"Something on your mind?" Rowan asked.

"No," he said, turning his attention back to the bastion he had to assault that night. "Not anymore."

5

Bolan scaled the walls at 2:00 a.m.

The trees on the left side of the pyramid-shaped pleasure palace gave him easy access to a second-floor balcony. From there he climbed hand over hand, pulling himself up cornerstones, walking on ledges, and now and then using a grappling hook to tug himself up to the next level.

The tines of the grappling hook were coated with rubber to soften any sound they made when they dug into the concrete ledges. And the hum of the air-conditioning units also helped to cover his approach.

Even with enough ambient noise to mask his climb, it still took Bolan almost thirty minutes to make it.

Though it was well past the witching hour, a number of hotel guests were still active. Several times the Executioner found himself clinging to the side of the building, an unintentional eavesdropper waiting for tipsy lovers to finish a last drink or a last embrace before drifting back into their hotel rooms. It was a night meant for looking at the stars, not at a man in black hauling himself up the side of their hotel. Things like that tended to make hotel guests sound the alarm.

Bolan made it to the top floor without incident. Almost.

Then he saw the sleeping man.

He'd just clambered over the edge of a fifth-floor balcony when he heard a strange wheezing and grunting sound. Part snoring, part death rattle. Bolan looked down. The unconscious giant was directly below him, passed out on a cushioned chaise lounge.

He was moving his head from side to side. Disturbed by the hook, Bolan thought. Or maybe it was the violent dreams of his past that caused him to stir.

He recognized the face. It was one of the colonel's men caught on the NSA footage with his boss.

The DOA gunman's apelike arms were spread out on both sides of him, knuckles scraping the floor. Bare chested and drunk from a long night of drinking and debauchery, he was surrounded by several bottles of booze, trays of room-service platters and a discarded nightgown from his professional paramour.

The girl was obviously sleeping it off inside. The broad-chested brute with a hedge of unkempt hair was more nightmare than dream date. His muscled body had gone to fat, and it was scarred with whip marks, old knife wounds and badly healed bullet wounds.

But he still was a danger. His revolver was just inches away from his hand, its handle jutting out from the holster. Even in this subconscious state he was still ready to protect his boss.

Bolan stood on the ledge, debating what to do. He didn't want to leave anyone behind in case he had to make a fast exit from the top floor. But he didn't want to risk waking any DOA troops before he had a chance to get to the colonel.

As if he were reading Bolan's thoughts, the gunman opened his eyes. He blinked, startled at the vision of the man in black. It took him only a fraction of a second to realize the apparition wasn't a figment of a bad dream. This was a long overdue payback. His hand reached for the gun.

By then Bolan was standing fully upright on the ledge with his outstretched hand pointed down at him.

The hushed shot from the Ram-Line Exactor pistol

thwacked into the target's skull, quickly flooding the entrance wound with a pool of blood.

Bolan immediately followed up with a second shot to the heart. The man sank back into the lounge cushions, permanently cured from whatever sleep disorder had racked his body.

For such a big man the two rounds weren't overkill. The Ram-Line Exactor was a lightweight .22-caliber pistol with a Precision Arms International suppressor. A stealth model that lived up to its name.

The weapon's sound-suppressed rounds were barely louder than the man's aggravated snoring had been. But the Executioner waited it out anyway, just to see if anyone had been alerted. He peered through the sliding glass doors that led into the hotel room.

Nothing was moving, and no sound was coming from any of the other floors. Bolan tucked the suppressed Exactor back into the Velcro harness. It was a solid piece, part of the package that Sandy Rowan had stowed aboard the Stinger. Bolan had a chance to burn off several rounds earlier in the day, knowing that his life depended on his familiarity with the weapon. Rowan had taken the boat on a run down the eastern side of Emerald Caye, where there were plenty of isolated spots to practice.

The Executioner was also carrying a compact version of the Walther P-88, a 9 mm pistol tucked into a small-of-the-back holster that kept it from snagging on his climbing rig. He would have preferred to have his own Beretta 93-R with him, but bringing it legally through customs would let a few people know he was here on more than business. The rig had stayed on Brognola's flight to the capital city. Since the big Fed was on official business, there would be no trouble unloading that kind of hardware from the plane. Eventually, the weapon would make its way back to the coast.

Bolan continued making his ascension, looping the

rubber-coated hook beyond the top balcony and letting it catch on the roof ledge. He tugged hard on the military spec cord, then swung a few feet into space.

His feet skipped across the harsh textured side of the building, following the pendulum like arc that brought him to the corner.

Anchored by the rooftop lifeline, he clamped the ascender onto the cord and walked a few steps up the side of the building, repeating the process until he reached the roof.

Bolan crept across the rooftop, carefully spreading out his steps to balance his weight and avoid alerting the sleepers below. He stopped at the sturdy metal base of the flagpole and wrapped the grappling hook around it, yanking hard to secure the cord.

He continued holding on to the rope as he neared the edge of the roof directly above the colonel's room. At the lip of the hotel bulwark he dropped into a crouch, a black-clad gargoyle surveying the grounds of the stylish Caribbean resort that was about to become a battleground.

Bolan scanned the dark vista of the sea with its temporary floating colony of wealthy visitors to Emerald Caye. The yachts and sailboats rocked up and down in the water, most of them with dim cabins, but there were a few boats that still had lights on. He imagined that in a very short time all the lights in the bay would flick on and the engines would roar into life.

He sought out the curved features of the bay off to his left, picking out the sheltered inlet where Rowan had moored the Stinger. It was close enough to the hotel so they could get away, but it was a fairly long run through the woods, especially if DOA pursuers were right behind.

The Executioner scrutinized the surroundings one more time, memorizing all of the possible escape routes. And then there was the absolute last resort six floors below. The swimming pool. A long shot if he had to jump for it. Maybe if he had time, maybe if no one was shooting at him, he could dive for it. But even then, the impact might knock him out and he'd be a sitting duck for anyone at poolside.

Screw it. He wasn't in the mood for a swim.

Drawing the cord tight, Bolan eased himself over the side and kept just enough tension on the shunt descender to glide to the terrace below.

As his feet touched the floor, he caught his reflection in the sliding glass doors. He looked through the image of the ghostly warrior splashed upon the glass and into the suite where the colonel and his latest conquest lay dreaming in oblivion.

He tried the handle with his left hand.

Locked.

Bolan removed the tube of embrittlement compound from his vest pocket and ran it up and down the metal seam, then spread it liberally around the locking mechanism. It produced an instant chemical reaction, foaming and churning through the slender strips of metal as it turned them into fragile corroded shells.

He grabbed the handle again with his left hand and pushed down while pressing his body against the glass frame. The lock gave way, and the glass panel slid free. A gust of ice hit Bolan in the face as the frigid air rushed out through the opening.

He slipped into the room and stopped to listen.

His entrance had interrupted the breathing of the two people in the room, triggering their preternatural instincts to let them know that something dangerous was about. He moved to one side of the room so his silhouette wouldn't loom above them if either one looked toward the window.

The girl was on the side of the bed closest to him. It was the same girl as before, the one who so splendidly decorated the terrace. The colonel was sleeping on his side, curled up and facing the other way. His body stirred uneasily, as if he were growing aware of the presence in the room but was still in the grip of Morpheus.

Bolan rested his hand on the uppermost edge of a long wet bar and used the support to muffle his footsteps as he stepped closer to the bed. Coke and smoke covered the top of bar. The colonel and his escort had sampled the wares that made his fortune.

A half dozen white lines of cocaine were spread out on a gold filigreed hand mirror. Several twisted joints of prime Central American cannabis were lined up along a heavy star-shaped ashtray.

These guys went overboard in everything they did, Bolan thought. There was enough there to waste an army. Which was good for Bolan, bad for the colonel. In this case a good high meant goodbye.

Bolan neared the bed, using the long blunt nose of the Exactor to lead the way. Though he didn't make a sound the girl suddenly gasped.

An alarm clock had gone off inside of her. A survival alarm.

She sat straight up and opened her mouth to scream. But she held it in check, mesmerized by the figure in black who stood over her with his face streaked with camouflage paint and ready for war.

Bolan's left hand shot up like a priest blessing a penitent. Instead of a blessing it was a warning. His index finger crossed his lips in the universal gesture for silence.

The girl's eyes went wide, looking first at his left hand, then at his right, which held a different kind of silencer entirely.

She nodded slowly and accepted the bargain. Whatever the man in black wanted, she would go along with. It was obvious this wasn't the first time she ever encountered a man with a gun. Especially if she hung around with this coarse kind of crew.

Bolan levitated her with his left hand, crooking his index finger to coax her out of the bed. Then he waved her over to the corner of the room toward a black lacquered armoire that offered her some semblance of safety.

For a moment he thought about gagging her and tying her up, but she might get the wrong idea and panic. He decided to trust her better judgment. After all, she was a professional and had no particular allegiance to the DOA crew. Right now her allegiance was to anyone who could get her out of this situation alive.

The Executioner didn't like running an operation where civilians were involved, but in this case there was no other way of doing it. His assignment was to get to Sandor before he had a chance to vanish. He was supposed to take him out for questioning, or if that proved impossible, just take him out.

The colonel might be having exactly the same idea, Bolan realized when he saw the man's body suddenly flinch as if his fight or flight instinct had just kicked in. It didn't mean he was awake, but as Bolan neared the side of the bed previously warmed by the Belizean party girl, he noticed that the colonel's hand was buried beneath the pillow much deeper than before.

Sandor's breathing seemed ordinary now. Too ordinary.

No one slept that easily, Bolan thought, particularly a man who had so much blood on his hands.

"Rosalind?" the man said, his voice muffled in the sheets. His left hand sprawled out and patted the bed next to him. "Where are you?"

"She's out of your reach, Colonel," Bolan said, pressing the end of the suppressor to the back of his head. He angled it at the base of the skull so it would plow a .22-caliber round up through his brain. "And for your sake I hope your gun's out of reach, too. I'd hate to kill you before we had a chance to talk."

"Yes," Sandor said. "We must talk."

Then he erupted from the bed, pushing up with both hands and suddenly pivoting on his left hand. He spun with an acrobatic grace that belied his out-of-shape body. It was born of sheer desperation, but at the end of the maneuver he had an arm lock hooked around Bolan's neck.

The colonel dropped as suddenly as he sprang up, using his deadweight to pull down on Bolan's head.

It was a good technique.

But the Executioner scooped the ashtray off the bar with his left hand, literally crowning the ex-army colonel. Stone spears shattered, and the jagged tray clawed into Sandor's scalp. He dropped forward and tumbled against the wall with a loud thud. Then he fell back on the bed.

Bolan lifted up the pillow.

Beneath it was a pistol, which he swept to the floor.

The Executioner realized he'd made a mistake by letting the colonel know that he wanted information. That gave the other man the split second necessary to make his move, knowing that Bolan would hesitate to kill him.

It was the kind of gamble that worked once.

"Hope it's out of your system, Colonel. Next time you catch one of these." Bolan gestured with the suppressed Exactor.

Sandor groaned. A moment ago he'd tried to take Bolan's life, now he looked like a beaten man, lying flat on his back with his outsized gut spilling over a pair of boxer shorts, and a bloody wound oozing down the front of his head. He leaned back against the headboard and staunched the blood with his palm.

"You understand your situation?" Bolan asked.

"I understand," the man groaned. "What do you want to know?"

"Let's start with Simon Liege's whereabouts."

The colonel looked shocked. "That name is familiar," he said. "But I can't place him."

"Try a little harder," Bolan suggested. "He happens to be the head of DOA. Maybe you can place him by thinking about the guy who was standing next to you on the Texas border not all that long ago. Remember? When you and the rest of those uniformed thugs murdered the Americans who were waiting for you."

Sandor nodded. "Oh," he said, aware that somehow his assailant had concrete knowledge of their activities. "Yes, I know him. But as for his whereabouts..." He shrugged. "He keeps that a secret from most of us. He either comes to us or summons us from wherever we are stationed."

"And then?"

"And then he gives our orders."

"Sounds possible," Bolan said. "So let's talk about where he stations you—"

The door to the hotel suite shook violently. Someone outside the room pounded on the door and tried to turn the knob. One or more of his men had been alerted by the sounds of the struggle.

"Colonel? Are you all right?"

Bolan held the suppressed pistol an inch from Sandor's forehead. Then he nodded rapidly at him, mimicking the response he wanted. The colonel got the message. "Yes!" he shouted out. "Nothing is wrong."

"We heard noise." The voice outside the room sounded drunk and surly, thirsting for violence.

"It's that Rosalind of mine," Sandor said, forcing himself to laugh through his bloodied lips. "She's a feisty one. We had a minor disagreement, but it's all over now. Go back to bed, Joaquim."

It was only there for a passing moment, but the crafty look on the colonel's face gave him away. Something he said tipped off the men outside the room. Joaquim, Bolan thought. The name was probably a distress signal.

A split second later the door flew off its hinges and smacked flat onto the floor with a loud thud. Two DOA troopers immediately charged into the room. One man dived straight onto the floor with his revolver held out in front of him. The other man darted into the room at an angle.

A blizzard of gunshots echoed inside the small hotel room. They were both firing wildly. One blast crashed through the sliding glass door. Another deafening shot punched a hole in the wall just above the colonel's head. He screamed and rolled off the bed.

Bolan was ready for both of the gunmen. As soon as they'd made their entry, he immediately picked out the most dangerous threat, the one who caught a glimpse of Bolan from his peripheral vision as he skidded across the floor. Now that he'd located a target, the crazed man might actually hit something. Bolan hit him first, drilling him three times with the Exactor. One head shot and two to the back. The man's head banged on the door and spattered it with a streak of blood.

The Executioner's left hand squeezed off two rounds from the Walther P-88 that he'd pulled from his back holster. The 9 mm slugs knocked the second DOA hitter back against the wall. He hung there for a moment as if the bullets had nailed him to the wood. Then he tumbled forward.

Bolan harnessed the suppressed weapon. There was no need for stealth anymore. Not when half of the hotel heard the gunshots.

And the screaming.

Rosalind was shrieking so loudly she was clamping her hands to her ears to block it out. She'd reached her limit for the night. So many bullets had gone off around her that she thought one was bound to find her eventually.

Bolan ignored her. His main concern was Sandor.

During the commotion, he'd rolled off the bed and was scurrying for the gun on the floor.

He found the gun. And that sealed his fate.

Bolan triggered the Walther. The P-88 projectile nailed him in the chest just above the heart and spun him with an extra nine millimeters of lead added to his bulk. The colonel's momentum brought his clenched gun hand around toward Bolan even as he was dying. The Executioner squeezed off another shot from the Walther, ripping apart the man's thick forearm.

The gun dropped to the floor and Sandor dropped even farther.

Bolan quickly stepped over to the entryway and listened for any sounds of approach. Nothing.

For the moment.

The colonel had six to eight men on the top two floors. Men who were probably drunk, stoned or terrified, or maybe all three at once. Any second now they'd be staggering around, shooting at ghosts.

Not good for the rest of the hotel guests, Bolan thought. The Executioner didn't want to endanger any of them. It was time to go.

He ran out to the terrace, grabbed the black cord that dangled from the flagpole and climbed over the side.

He abseiled to the fifth floor, kicking off when he got to the edge. He sailed out into space again and sought purchase on the fourth-floor terrace. He moved quickly down to the next floor.

A startled hotel guest ran out to the terrace just as he touched down on the edge. She ran back inside screaming.

Bolan pushed off again. Then he saw the bright barrel-flash of a suppressed submachine gun as it spit a burst of lead his way. The bullets burned the air around him, then torpedoed into the pool below.

Bolan saw the shape on the sixth floor taking aim at him

again just as he was about to drop from the ledge. Instead of making a wide arc the Executioner slid straight down like a spider on a string, avoiding the bullet stream.

He was dangling in the air, suspended between floors on the harness rig, when three more rounds suddenly ripped from the trees on the side of the hotel.

Bolan spun to see the new threat. The motion swung him back and forth like a pendulum and offered an easy target for whoever was shooting from the ground. He looped one hand around the cord to steady himself and dug out the Walther with his other hand. He was aiming the 9 mm pistol toward the trees when another trio of flashes flamed up through the woods again.

The fact that he was still alive made him realize he wasn't the intended target.

The bullets climbed up the front of the sixth-floor terrace, homing in on the DOA gunman. A follow-up burst scythed through the gunman's chest and knocked him out of view. His automatic weapon pinwheeled in the air and clattered on the ground below.

Rowan unleashed another volley of suppressing fire from her position in the woods, covering Bolan while he touched down on the rim of the second-floor terrace.

Bolan left the grappling rope hanging in space and sprinted to the corner edge of the terrace. He caught a flash of motion on the ground below and saw one of the colonel's men running along the side of the swimming pool.

"There he is!" the man shouted. "Take him!" The poolside gunman ripped off a full-auto burst that chewed into the ledge beneath Bolan's feet and sent a stinging spray of concrete into his legs.

Before the next tracking rounds came his way the Executioner went airborne, diving toward the shadowy tree line that almost brushed against the hotel.

He came down hard on a thick limb that knocked the

wind out of him, clinging to it by instinct. He ignored the crushing pain in his chest and clambered for the relative safety of the tree trunk.

The man by the pool got off another burst and shredded the treetops above Bolan before an answering burst from Rowan's Heckler & Koch took him out. A second poolside gunner ran for cover when he saw his partner fall.

Bolan gripped a branch fifteen feet off the ground, picked out a moonlight patch of earth, then swung out and let go. He dropped to the earth with a loud thump and landed almost at Rowan's feet.

"You okay?" she said, surveying the soldier as he straightened.

"Haven't been killed once," he said, remembering the phrase she'd used earlier when she thought he was questioning her ability.

"Let's keep it that way," she replied. "Boat's over there." She pointed through the thick mass of forest to the hidden shoreline.

Two minutes later the Chris-Craft Stinger joined the chaotic armada that had come to life in Emerald Caye. All around them engines were growling into life, running lights were flicking on and worried boaters were shouting to one another across the water, trying to find out what was going on.

Above the chaotic din Bolan heard the words terrorist attack echoing across the water. The phrase was repeated from boat to boat.

Terrorists attacked, Bolan thought as they quickly threaded their way through the boats and made a run for it. Lights off, night-vision goggles on.

Ten minutes later, when they were alone in the open sea, Bolan used the Stinger's secure communications gear to reach Hal Brognola back at the mainland capital. "It's done," Bolan said when the head Fed came on the secure line. "Send in the troops to take a few more shots at the opposition."

The *troops* were the media in Belize City, television and newspaper reporters eager for a story that would put them on the map. Brognola's Agency people had identified their key contacts in the sophisticated Belizean press. With the right spin, the reporters' shots would be heard and seen around the world.

6

The mud-covered caravan of Land Rovers bounced and jostled down the last mile of narrow road, roof racks littered with jungle debris from plowing through one of the densest rain forests in all of Belize. Each driver gripped the wheel tightly to navigate through the bone-jarring ruts and ravines left behind by the recent flash flood.

Simon Liege rode in the lead SUV, and he was just as mud spattered as the rest of the men. They'd used a combination of winches, tow ropes and old-fashioned solid muscle to push and pull the off-road vehicles out of the various entanglements they'd fallen into.

They'd been traveling for ten miles across washed-out stretches of road, now and then having to float the vehicles on inflatable braces specially made for the Land Rovers. It wasn't an easy ride even during the dry season. That was one of the advantages of the isolated encampment they were heading for.

Located in a mostly unsettled corner of Belize, with Mexico to the north and Guatemala to the west, the Alacan Institute wasn't the kind of place someone idly wandered into. But it was exactly the kind of place where Simon Liege could hide in plain sight. It was owned by a holding company that operated several other forest preserves and research institutes scattered across the country.

It was a perfect cover. Eco-tours and rain forest resorts were one of the fastest-growing businesses in Central America, particularly in Belize where there was so much virgin territory to explore. Scientists, journalists and student interns often visited the country to study the flora and fauna, explore the underwater cave systems, or look for Mayan ruins that were believed to occupy the area.

Another attraction of Belize was its relative stability compared to the neighboring countries that had been fighting civil wars for thirty years or more. These days the main threat to Belize came from its much larger Guatemalan neighbor, which periodically threatened to annex Belize whenever the military leader of the time felt the need to rattle his sabers.

It was all part of the grand machismo theater in the area. In previous years whenever Guatemalan troops massed on the border with Belize, SAS units flew in from Britain and dropped from the sky on training maneuvers, landing within shouting and shooting distance of the Guatemalans. Thousands of British commandos would take boat trips through the rivers that spiderwebbed the Belizean interior and flowed into Guatemala. At the same time, the British navy would conduct maneuvers off the Belizean coast with ships in striking range of the Guatemalan interior.

In those days the Guatemalans always backed down. Now that the American Special Forces were the official advisers to the BDF, the Guatemalan military had backed off. They remembered all too well the American invasions into Grenada and Panama. All things considered, Alacan was a safe harbor for DOA operations.

The rain forest complex was in a class all by itself. It was a former radar tower operated by the British SAS to monitor the drug trafficking air corridors from Colombia and Peru. When the U.K. troops left Belize, the tower was abandoned and quickly fell into a state of disrepair.

The new owners reclaimed it from the jungle and turned it into a rain forest resort that hosted students, scientists and tourists. At least on paper. In reality most visitors to the site were members of the DOA. Now and then Liege had one of his caretakers host a genuine tour group just to make it look legal. But those trips were few and far between.

Despite the logos on the Land Rover's side panels, complete with Alacan's proud slogan A World in Need of Saving, not a single member of this convoy was part of a tour group. Instead they were a hard-core cadre of mercenaries personally recruited and refined by Liege over the years. His palace guard.

Liege's SUV broke through the clearing at the end of the road, then rolled across the high grass and parked right next to the tower. The rest of the vehicles pulled up alongside the outbuildings that served as dormitories or barracks, depending upon the need. The totally self-sufficient compound, complete with generators and satellite dishes, was outfitted with enough supplies to last for several months.

Liege was the first one out of his SUV. His boots sank into the marshy ground by the base of the tower as he surveyed the compound. Fresh tire tracks showed where a bulldozer blade had gouged out a safety zone between the rain forest and the cleared land around the tower.

"God, it's hotter than hell out here," said Aaron Priestly, his second in command, who caught up to him after barking orders to the troops unloading the vehicles. The man was pushing fifty, a mutton-chopped gent from the old school who still played the mercenary's game, even though he always complained it was a younger man's racket.

Liege smiled. He was used to the heat, the hot humid breath that constantly radiated from the jungle. The trick wasn't to fight it, but to accept it. Move a bit slower until the time came for action. No matter how long he was down here, Liege knew that Priestly would never get used to it.

"Don't die on me yet," Liege said, looking at the huffing

and puffing hulk beside him. "We've got work to do. Let's go inside and get some fresh air."

"Right behind you, Simon," Priestly said.

Liege nodded at Sergeant Eric Knoll, the caretaker who was standing on the second-floor landing outside the tower. He was armed and he was at attention. Old habits died hard with that one, Liege thought.

Knoll was a former member of the Belizean Defense Force. He'd caught Liege's attention from his first day as a recruit when he knocked his would-be combat instructor cold with a move no one had even seen. Liege had mentored him from that day on. Now he was a seasoned member of DOA, an advance man for Liege's operations. Along with a small skeleton staff, the efficient trooper kept the site free of intruders.

"Everything's ready, sir," the caretaker reported as Liege climbed up the stairs. "We bulldozed enough space for the helicopter this morning. My men are scouting the perimeter."

"We didn't see them on the way in, Sergeant," Liege said.

"That's the idea, sir," he replied, tossing him a crisp salute reminiscent of their days together when they were a legitimate fighting force.

Knoll held the door open for Liege and Priestly.

Once inside the complex they walked up another steep flight of stairs and emerged into a loftlike canopy that seemed to be made mostly of glass. Following the fashion of most rain forest resorts, its walls were replaced by glass panels or sliding doors that made the guests feel as if they were an intimate part of the surroundings. The floors and ceilings were made of natural wood to enhance the effect.

An altarlike table of polished gray stone occupied the center of the room. It was surrounded by tall ladder-back chairs with elegantly carved armrests. Ceiling vents above the table piped cool air into the room, reviving Priestly as quickly as a blood transfusion.

Liege and Priestly each grabbed a chair and sat at the long table, sipping afternoon tea while they waited for their guest to arrive.

Within a half hour they heard the first thrumming of the helicopter as it flew low across the treetops. The chopper came in from the north, flew around the tower once to check out the landing zone, then kicked up a tornado of dirt and tall grass as it settled softly on the ground.

It was a sleek combat scout gunship. American issue. Part of the matériel that had been given to the Mexican military to help them in their counter drug operations. Like most U.S. military hardware donated to the drug war, it quickly found its way into the hands of the drug lords. The army and the police simply acted as brokers.

Jorge Macedonio jumped out of the cabin and hurried toward the tower, reducing the amount of time he was a target to anyone in the area. The second man out of the chopper had to run to keep up with him.

Macedonio's pilot kept the engines running in case he had to make a fast exit. Though he had grown into a powerful and feared man, Macedonio was still as paranoid as the day he first started out. It was a natural state of mind for someone who had killed his share of partners on the bloody climb to the top. He knew too well that sooner or later someone would follow his example and try to take him out.

Liege watched through the glass as Knoll led the newcomers up the staircase outside the tower. When they reached the top floor Liege stepped forward to personally greet them at the door, then led them to the center of the room.

Macedonio took a seat at the end of the table opposite from Liege and helped himself to a generous shot of tequila from the silver service tray Knoll had placed by him. Tea, tequila, bottled water, beer, coffee. Whatever it took to get through their meeting was available on the table.

The heavily armed bodyguard who accompanied Macedonio from the helicopter stood with his back to the window and silently watched the proceedings. He had the impassive and unconcerned stare of a man who was prepared to take out everyone in the room if necessary. Or die trying.

It was a perfect complement to the omnipotent stare of Knoll, who stood at the window across from the bodyguard. They were just like pieces on a cartel chessboard, Liege thought, as he watched the two men stare at each other. And he and Macedonio were the kings, lean and dangerous men willing to impose their wills upon the world.

"Thank you for coming all this way," Liege said.

Macedonio nodded. "We have much planning to do, my friend," he said. "It's better to do it here. All this talk of DOA in the news gives me an incentive to travel. Too much heat in my country at the moment."

Liege was surprised at the undercurrent in the other man's voice. It almost sounded as if Macedonio were spooked. "Surely you can't be worried about the police. Or the army?"

"Of course not," Macedonio said. "But with the eyes of the world upon them, they must pretend to do their job. They demand a higher price for protection in times of crisis."

"It hasn't reached the crisis stage yet," Liege said.

"No? First there is the news about Emerald Caye. All over the papers and the television. DOA terrorists killed in gun battle. They linked these so-called terrorists to the battle at Del Rio. And to me."

"It's just the usual propaganda," Liege said. "The spin doctors try to divert attention from themselves and sow dissension in our ranks. It's the most basic approach."

"Basic or not," Macedonio said. "I was named."

The DOA leader shrugged. "Sandor was your man."

"At one time, yes," Macedonio said. "But then he became *our* man. And now he is gone."

"And we are all of us quite saddened indeed," Priestly said, leaning forward and speaking for the first time since the two leaders began their conference. "He was a good man." He sipped his tea and sat back, satisfied with his impromptu split-second eulogy.

Macedonio shot the older British merc a look. "You despised him," he said. "I heard you say so many times."

Priestly nodded. "As a matter of fact I did," he said. "But nonetheless he was still a good man to have on your side. He knew the right palms to grease and he knew where a lot of skeletons were buried."

"And now he joins them," Macedonio said, permitting himself a sad smile at the colonel's expense. "Poor Arturo." He tossed down a shot of tequila and shrugged, having used up his allotted share of sorrow. "I'll have to find someone to take his place. Until then I'll personally manage some of my business affairs. But our real problem remains. How did they know Arturo was involved at all? How did they connect him to the Texas operation?"

"The Americans have an extremely advanced surveillance capacity, perhaps ten years ahead of anyone else in the business," Liege said. "Despite what they tell the world, they don't share their technology with their Western allies until it is obsolete and they've moved on to the next generation."

The Mexican cartel chief wasn't convinced. "No matter how advanced they are, they're not mind readers."

"Not yet," Priestly said. "But believe me, they're working on it."

"I know both of you are impressed with American technology," Macedonio said. "But how did they know where to cast the net? What if there's a leak in our organization?"

Liege shook his head. "There's nothing to worry about," he said. "They either had that area of the border under constant surveillance and called up the data afterward or someone in their group was suspicious of the handoff and set up a special watch just for us."

"But how do they know who was involved? They identified Arturo so quickly."

"They can identify just about anyone these days. Big Brother's been and gone, and been replaced by an even better apparatus. Somehow that apparatus tracked Arturo to his hotel."

"Bloody fool should have kept a low profile," Priestly said.

Macedonio raised his eyebrows and gave Priestly a stare that would have made a lesser man contemplate the afterlife. "A moment ago you said he was a good man."

"A good man," Priestly agreed. "But a foolish one. He and his crew were more interested in getting laid than staying alive."

Macedonio nodded. "That brings me to the second bit of distressing news. There have been more deaths."

Liege nodded his acknowledgment. "We heard about the trouble at Four Square."

Macedonio nodded. "The ranch was part of a much larger operation set up by my people in the north," he said. "It was turned into a ghost town. All of our people gone. All of their vehicles gone. The media said it was a falling out among thieves. And once again my name was linked to it. If not for one of the Americans who made it out alive, we wouldn't know what really happened."

"I'd like to have one of my people debrief him," Liege said.

"That could be difficult," Macedonio replied. "He was

questioned thoroughly about why he was the only one who managed to escape. Too thoroughly. He didn't survive—but told us everything he could.'' Macedonio filled them in on the attack on the ranch. How a crew of machine-gun cowboys went out to take down a single man who'd strayed onto their land. And none of them made it back.

"One man?" Liege asked. "Are you sure?"

"He was picked up on their sensors. Think about it, my friends. A solitary man. Just like the one who hit Emerald Caye. In fact, it could be the same man."

"Let's hope it is," Liege said. "We're already working on him."

Priestly looked surprised at the news.

Liege smoothed his hands out on the table. "We studied the news reports on the hotel hit. Even sent one of our people posing as a reporter. He paid the witnesses extremely well for their description of this man."

Macedonio looked impressed. "You have his identity?"

"No," Liege said.

"If you don't know his name—"

"We know his occupation," Liege said. "Executioner. This man fits the pattern of the ones used by the U.S. government on sensitive operations. Like Del Rio, like Emerald Caye, like a dozen other operations."

"How can you stop such a man?"

"We have an executioner of our own," Liege said. "A man named Carvaggio. He's done the same kind of work for the Mob. That's why I brought him onboard. If it really is a special ops agent behind these attacks, he'll stay right here in Belize and come looking for us."

"And that is a good thing?" Macedonio asked.

Liege nodded. "Carvaggio will let himself be found."

"Where is this Carvaggio now?"

Liege turned toward his second in command. "Priestly keeps tabs on Carvaggio and some of our other specialists.

Right after our meeting, he's going to send him after his opposite number.''

"That's welcome news," Macedonio said. "But we still must deal with the damage done to our enterprise. Already I have heard word from our benefactors. Some of the very same men who championed our cause now wish to run and hide. They think DOA is a mistake that will bring ruin to us all.''

"We'll have to show them it's not.''

"How?''

"By striking back at the enemy," Liege said. "That's why we're here today.'' He reached inside his deep shirt pocket and removed a sheet of paper. He unfolded it carefully, smoothed out the wrinkles and dropped it on the table.

It was a list of names and locations.

"What's that?'' Macedonio asked.

"That's our proposed order of battle," Liege said. He nodded to Priestly, who slid it down to Macedonio's end of the table.

The cartel chief read the names, shaking his head.

"This is like war.''

"It is war," Liege said. "All-out war. Let's see how the American feel about continuing their raids on our people when they see that their own borders are no longer safe.''

THE ST. GEORGE BAR and Hotel in the southern Belizean village of New Albion wasn't really a bordello according to Christine Bright, the well-built, well-traveled brunette who ran the place. Helping her out was a staff of British expatriates who followed their dreams and somehow ended up at the doors of her hotel.

Bright thought of the St. George as a free enterprise zone for some very enterprising girls who liked to hang out all hours of the day or night. If the girls wanted to work out arrangements with newfound friends they met in the bar, that was their business. If they decided to provide her with a generous tip every time they rented a room, that was their business, too.

The girls ranged from ex-au pairs to refugees to local girls gone bad. Everyone was welcome provided they didn't make too much trouble.

These days business was better than ever at the St. George. The small riverside hamlet of New Albion always had a steady stream of visitors. But ever since the owner of the hotel brought in a construction crew to start work on a projected rain forest resort just outside of town, the hotel was under siege by a hard drinking and fast spending crew.

The men were quartered throughout the town, taking up most of the available lodging in the two long streets of brightly painted homes and hostels that made up New Albion. During their off hours they practically lived at the St. George.

One of the most frequent residents was a man named Nicholas, a strapping man who kept to himself most of the time, when he wasn't dodging the attentions of the St. George girls.

He came into the hotel shortly after five o'clock and took his usual place at the end of the bar. Before any of the girls could corner him, Bright drifted over to his side. She spread her arms and leaned over the counter, giving him a killer smile and a glimpse of cleavage at the same time.

"Hello, Nicky," she said. "You're early, today."

"Early? I haven't gone to sleep yet. I just got your message."

"Good man," she said. "Glad to see you're still living the high life. I wouldn't want you going soft on me."

"That would never happen."

Bright laughed, brushing her long black hair back over her shoulders. "I'll be the judge of that, Nicky. When you and I finally get around to it."

"Oh? Is that why you sent for me? They told me it was urgent."

"Afraid not," she said. She jerked her head toward the rear of the bar that led to her private offices. "He's here."

"Another time?"

"You know where to find me."

He drifted through the back of the hotel and climbed a short flight of steps into her private office.

Aaron Priestly, the silent owner of the St. George Bar and Hotel, sat behind Bright's desk looking like a plump vulture on a leather-clad perch.

"Sit down, Nick," he said. "I've got a proposition for you."

"Thanks, but I just had one," Carvaggio said, pulling the wheeled chair away from the desk and settling into it. "Turned it down."

"You'll accept this proposition," Priestly said. "No doubt about that."

"What makes you so sure?"

"Simon Liege wanted the best man for this kind of thing. That narrows it down to you. I don't think he'll accept a refusal."

"What's the gig?"

"A chance to make your way in the organization, Nick. Rise through the ranks and all that. Become part of his private cadre."

"Who do I have to kill?"

"Right to the point," Priestly said. "Good. We're talking about a man sorely in need of killing. A man who very efficiently killed Sandor and his men on Emerald Caye."

"He killed them all?" Carvaggio asked.

"Yes, he did. Or he scared them away. Not a single DOA man came back from the island—KIA, MIA, deserter, whatever their status, he's responsible. From all accounts he's a special ops type. Extremely resourceful, extremely high caliber. A man such as yourself.''

"Who is he?''

"We're not exactly sure," Priestly said. "But he acts like an executioner.''

Carvaggio was stunned by the news. "You can't be serious," he said.

Priestly laughed at his reaction, misinterpreting his surprise for fear. "Don't worry, you'll have plenty of help.''

"An executioner," Carvaggio mused.

"So we believe. And if you believe what you see on the telly, he's going to put DOA out of business and make the world spin right on its axis again. From what we've seen so far, he just may be able to do it.''

Carvaggio nodded. "So I hear.''

"Do you accept?''

"Yes. Provided you meet my conditions.''

"Name them.''

Carvaggio ticked off his fingers. "I'll need spending money. A lot of it. A couple of safehouses, vehicles at my disposal, passports, contacts, the works.''

"You'll have it," he said. "Within reason. Don't want you flying off to the Riviera, do we?''

"And one more thing,''

"What's that?''

"I want to talk to Liege personally," Carvaggio said. "So far I've only seen him a couple of times, on the day I signed up and during the operation in Colombia.''

"Standard security precautions," Priestly said. "Simon keeps a low profile and is seen only by those who have good reason. But if you carry this off, you'll be one of them.''

"I want to see him before I take the assignment.''

"Afraid that's out of the question.''

"Why?''

"He's just left the country."

"Where is he?"

Priestly hesitated about parceling out such privileged information. Since Carvaggio was being groomed for the inner circle he relented. "Why he's gone to see America," he said.

7

The fishing boat glided along the north side of the rocky peninsula that jutted into the cold Atlantic waters off the Maine coast. Onboard were three Americans and five British nationals, all carrying fake passports and an assortment of lethal weaponry.

They also had a Zodiac inflatable raft that was lowered into the water two miles away from the Land's End lighthouse at the very tip of the peninsula.

The sky was dark and the waters were rough. Optimum conditions for the mission.

Simon Liege and four of his men began the slow approach toward the target. The modified engine piloting the inflatable was virtually silent, all noise drowned out by the roiling waves.

He knew it was a risky venture, just as his second in command had told him, but it was a risk he had to take. Liege couldn't pass up the chance to strike behind enemy lines. After the debacle at Emerald Caye, DOA needed a victory.

This mission would be both a political and military victory. If he survived it. If Priestly's warnings hadn't jinxed them.

Priestly had said over and over that they couldn't afford to lose the leader of DOA. To which Liege replied, if he couldn't survive the mission, then he wasn't fit to be the leader.

Liege still believed in the old-fashioned idea that he would never send his men out to do anything he couldn't do himself.

The Zodiac stayed close to the shore as it plowed through the choppy water. Chances were slim that anyone would see them. The closest sign of civilization was an artists' colony and fishing village several miles back, near the thick base of the peninsula. Only a handful of lights gleamed from the distant buildings.

The men were silent as they motored toward the part of the peninsula they had studied during a recon run earlier in the day. During the daylight it looked like a rock garden, with only a few patches of grass. At night it looked like a lonesome graveyard.

THE LIGHTHOUSE was dark, a tall silhouetted ghost of the days when it had actually served as a beacon for ships sailing the cold and dangerous waters for which Maine was known. These days it was just an artifact, a bit of impeccably kept historical landscaping.

The lighthouse and surrounding grounds had attracted a succession of New Englanders, including a couple who turned the lighthouse into a bed-and-breakfast until they realized they really didn't like having people stay in their home. They turned around and sold it to the current owner, Stephen Allred, a man whose face was once well known to the American public.

Allred was a former director of the Drug Enforcement Administration. He was often seen on network news programs and C-SPAN making the case for increasing military aid to Central and South American countries. His constant refrain was that it was time for the American people to get serious about the drug war.

As a former covert operator who led countless raids against Colombian processing labs and the Marxist guerrillas who controlled the countryside, Allred knew it was a failed policy. Most of the time the traffickers and guerrillas had advance knowledge about any raid from the Colombian military. In every sense of the word, the busts turned out to be real busts.

But the U.S. administration always wanted to claim a victory in the drug war, no matter how hollow. So Allred went along. He became the architect of a Pan-American antidrug alliance that spent almost a billion dollars per year with very little to show for it. Except for a few bodies now and then, mostly low-level traffickers or peasants caught in the cross fire, there were few real casualties in the war. But that didn't matter as long as he produced some good photos to saturate the American press with. Destroyed drug labs, burning coca fields, scorched marijuana plantations. They always made it to the front pages and helped Allred win the PR war.

After years of inflated claims about the great strides he was making in the drug war, Allred retired as a conquering hero. He sat on several corporate boards, wrote his memoirs.

And now he led an idyllic existence at his Maine coastal retreat, an elder statesman who was still sought out by network news crews whenever they wanted an informed opinion about the drug problem.

But this night as he slept soundly in his bed, he was being sought out by a different kind of crew.

LIEGE'S MEN landed in a small inlet fifty yards from the dock. They hauled the Zodiac onto the rocky incline and secured the rope line around a dolmen-shaped boulder.

They rapidly clambered up the massive slabs of stone that were clustered around the ridge in steplike formations, then fanned out across the lighthouse complex.

The five black shapes moved unseen and unheard, carrying short-barreled automatic weapons as they took up their positions.

One man sidled up to the covered walkway that led up to the old lighthouse. The others spread out around the attached cottage and sealed off all of the possible exits.

Liege took up position closest to Allred's bedroom, where several white trimmed windows looked out upon the ocean.

Allred lay inside, dead to the world.

Liege stepped away from the window until he was in line of sight of the next man and signaled that he had the target and was going in. He flashed ten fingers once, twice, letting them know he was going inside in twenty seconds.

He waited for the signal to make its way around the stone cottage. Then he announced his presence by tapping on the window with the blunt end of the Heckler & Koch's suppressor.

It took several taps before Allred stirred from his bed.

The wise old man of the covert community sat up in bed and immediately glanced toward the window.

As soon as he saw the silhouette outside his window, Allred jumped to his feet and reached for the bedside drawer.

Liege fired a burst from the Heckler & Koch. The 9 mm rounds smashed through the glass, turning the drawer into an exploding shower of splinters.

Allred staggered back and ran down the hall in his silk pajamas.

After smashing the remaining panes of glass and latticework with the gun barrel, Liege vaulted through the window and into the room.

He heard shouting from the front of the cottage. Allred was screaming at one of the DOA troopers.

Liege entered just in time to see the former covert operator in action. He'd picked up an iron poker from the fireplace and was slashing it like a club at one of Liege's men. The DOA trooper took a step back and held his weapon over his head as if he were pressing a barbell. The hooked bar of iron crashed down into the barrel with a loud whack. It held. And it trapped the poker long enough for the trooper to push up suddenly, toppling Allred backward.

Which was part of Allred's plan.

Allred continued falling until he was in reach of his gun cabinet. He smashed his fist through the glass, leaving behind several strips of flesh as he clenched his fist around a shotgun barrel.

Liege stepped forward and fired a burst into Allred's back.

The man slumped to the floor, his head resting on the broken glass, groaning. Liege triggered another burst and finished him off.

He turned to the other DOA troopers who'd gathered in the room. "Let them know we were here."

Liege pointed his sound-suppressed subgun at the large-screen television in the side of the room and blew it to pieces. His men moved up and down the rooms, gunning down paintings, blasting apart sculptures and tapestries, all of the treasures Allred had accumulated in his privileged life.

They sifted through his office, taking the hard drive from his computer, scooping up a batch of disks and breaking into his wall safe.

Just before they left, Liege walked back to Allred's desk and flipped open his leather-bound appointment book.

Then he wrote down Allred's last appointment on earth in large block letters: DOA.

8

Night fell a few hours earlier than usual, ushered in by the billowing black thunder clouds that rolled over the lonely stretch of Belizean coastline south of the Yucatán peninsula.

Patches of sun still shone through some of the clouds, but the darkening sky covered most of the horizon.

It was just another day in paradise for Felix Tomasa, the leader of the Belize National Police's elite Dragon Unit, a special operations team that worked closely with the U.S. Customs on maritime drug interdictions. The BDU was the Belizean version of U.S. Navy SEALs.

Tomasa's twin hull speedboat bobbed up and down alongside the houseboat and yachts moored at the Agency's elaborately constructed private dock complex. His three-man crew waited inside the twin-engined 575 hp pursuit craft while he headed for his sit-down with Mike Belasko.

Bolan's first glimpse of him was a silhouetted figure battering his way against the shrieking wind that kicked up miniature cyclones of sand along the freshly raked beach.

On most days the Company's seaside villa where Bolan was temporarily billeted looked like a five-star resort. This day it looked like an outpost at the edge of the world.

A dark blotch of sky trolled above the approaching Dragon headman as if it were his own private cloud of doom. He yanked off his camouflage headband to keep it from blowing away, then trekked across the sand with the zigzag steps of someone who'd lived through a lot of hurricane seasons. The kind of hurricanes that forced the Belizean government to move the seaside capital from Belize City to Belmopan in the interior.

From Mack Bolan's point of view inside the glass-sheltered terrace, the copper-toned bantamweight in khaki shorts didn't look very menacing. His unbuttoned shirt flapped in the wind like a kite about to take him aloft.

His hair was cut short, and from a distance he looked barely out of his teens. Definitely not a substantial looking man.

But the fact that he was the leader of the Dragon Unit spoke volumes. If he wasn't a capable man, the BDU team would waste no time in throwing him back. As with special forces units around the world, they chose the man they would follow.

The Dragon team had served with distinction in several paramilitary operations carried out by the American-sponsored RSS. As a multinational task force, the Regional Security System handled hostage rescue operations, stabilized governments during Caribbean coup season and played a large role in counter drug operations. Though the comparatively small Dragon Unit was often outnumbered by their allies on those joint operations, it was seldom outfought. The reason why was the man walking across the sand.

The Executioner had seen his type plenty of times before. Men whose outward stature was dwarfed by their willpower and ability to push their bodies beyond the limits. These were the kind of men who won wars.

Tomasa slipped through the glass doors and quickly shut them to seal out the battering wind. He stood there for a moment with his back to the shuddering glass while he surveyed the room. Then he studied Bolan, nodding as if the Executioner's presence matched up with the image he had in mind.

Up close Tomasa looked a bit more formidable. There was a knife strapped to an ankle sheath just above his canvas shoes. He also had a web belt with a side holster just barely hidden beneath the tails of his long shirt. Though he was slender, every bit of him was made of sinewy muscle.

He smiled as he approached the table where Bolan sat with a shot glass of whiskey, enjoying one of those rare moments when he had an opportunity to kick back.

Tomasa met him with an outstretched hand, and Bolan shook it. The grip was strong and quick. Just like the rest of him.

"Welcome to my country," Tomasa said.

"Thanks," Bolan said. "Actually, I've been here for a while."

"So I've heard."

The soldier cocked an eyebrow.

"My people keep tabs on everyone who visits this quaint little…retirement community," Tomasa said.

"Retirement?"

"Just an educated guess," Tomasa replied. "I haven't met a single person here who wasn't retired from the military, or an intelligence unit."

Bolan laughed. "Guess I qualify at that." Just about everyone who was staying at the villa was officially retired from active service with the military, the Department of State, or the intelligence community.

The villa on the coastal road that led to Belize City was one of the Company's unofficial stations, a clearinghouse for spooks and spec ops personnel moving through the area. It was staffed by people who had deniability in case any of their activities blew up and brought some flak down on the official station at the embassy.

The CIA ghost station came complete with a ghost chief of station, who, true to form, was rarely seen unless someone had personal business with him. Bolan's business was over. The station chief had taken an immediate dislike to him once he figured out that in the scheme of things Bolan had more pull than he would ever have. He'd tried to quarantine Bolan to the villa and control his movements in Belize—until Bolan handed him a satellite phone and said, "Talk to this man."

The man on the other end of the line had been Hal Brognola, and the big Fed made it clear that he was speaking for the White House, for God above and for any other metaphysical entity the station chief might care to believe in. The station chief nodded several times during the conversation while throwing daggers at Bolan with his eyes. When he disconnected the call he turned to Bolan and said, "For the record, you have my full cooperation."

Bolan nodded and said, "And in real life?"

The COS burned his gaze into Bolan. "In real life you fuck up one time, I'll bury you."

The Executioner was used to that kind of cooperation. Although they were all supposed to be fighting the same war, some people worked with him, some worked against him. It didn't matter. With or without them, he'd reach his objective.

However, the station chief had one redeeming quality. He never went anywhere without his friend JD. Along with local beers and rum, the bar was well stocked with plenty of Jack Daniel's whiskey. Bolan poured a shot for Tomasa and slid it across the table.

"You know," Tomasa said, "we had a few other indications that you—or someone like you was here."

"Such as?"

"The incident at the hotel on the caye. The media had a field day with it. Things like that just don't happen here. That's why it was all over the papers. Especially *The Belize Standard*."

"Yeah," Bolan said. "I read their coverage."

"Good paper," Tomasa said, "if a bit sensational. Made it sound like a terrorist civil war."

"Worked for me."

"It was a perplexing case at first. We had no doubt the target was involved in cartel activity—the girls, the goon squad, the fancy living, the kind of things those guys just can't seem to live without."

"And sometimes they die because of them," Bolan said, remembering how the man's high profile had left a trail that could be followed. The colonel wanted the world to see what a powerful man he was, flaunting his wealth and his entourage. Because of that he was now just a bad memory.

"Exactly," Tomasa agreed. "Initial reports indicated that it was a cartel hit. But then we learned the deceased was a DOA lieutenant suspected of involvement in the assault on the Texas border. He'd traveled down through Mexico, then came across the border to enjoy the fruits of his labors."

"Just like a conquering hero," Bolan said. "Coming home for some well deserved R and R."

"That was his plan," Tomasa said. "But someone scaled the walls, took him out, took out some of his people, and then made like Spiderman on his way back down. He took off swinging through the trees. Now this is the part that didn't get into the papers. We heard from our sources that there was a woman working with him, providing cover and helping him get away. A beautiful woman by all accounts."

"Sounds like a lucky guy," the soldier said.

"Unfortunately, his luck may not hold."

"How do you mean?"

"Officially we're supposed to be looking for that guy. Some people in the higher echelons of government believe the Americans are turning our country into the Wild West. They want to send him packing."

"And you?" Bolan asked.

"I welcome all the help I can get," he said. "But right now I need someone with smaller footprints."

The soldier nodded. "That's why Brognola wanted us to meet. To coordinate future activities. I understood you were the man in charge of joint ops."

The Dragon Unit commander drummed his fingers on the table. "Correct. Once a mission is launched I am in command. However, to get it launched is a different matter entirely. That decision is not always up to me."

Bolan sat back in his chair and studied Felix Tomasa. It was all in the eyes. They had the look of someone who had seen war up close, both the life-and-death kind and the bureaucratic. Now he had to fight another paperwork battle before he could zero in on the real enemy.

"We went through the chain of command," Bolan said. "You were identified as the primary contact."

"Officially I am," Tomasa said. "Our mutual friend, Mr. Brognola, can count on me in most circumstances. Unfortunately, this is a situation where other people have a say in what I do. One man in particular. Much of our support depends on this man."

"Who is he?"

"His name is St. Clair."

"Sounds familiar." Bolan searched his memory, sifting through the roster of names he'd seen on Brognola's dossiers. Then it came to him. Alexander St. Clair. He remembered a photograph that showed a distinguished looking statesman type. Tanned, coiffed, tuxedoed. A prominent player who was put out to pasture. "Okay, I know who you're talking about. But according to our briefings he hasn't been active for years."

"Ahh," Tomasa said, "the joys of retirement. St. Clair is retired in much the same way you are. The éminence grise in our covert apparatus. Some people say he has more power now than he ever did when he was active. Perhaps too much power."

Bolan didn't bother to hide his surprise. He'd been briefed extensively on the current power brokers in Belize, and until now St. Clair didn't fit into the equation. But who would know better than someone like the leader of the Dragon Unit?

"How about you, Felix?" Bolan asked. "Would you say he has too much power?"

Tomasa shook his head. "I wouldn't say it out loud," he replied. "St. Clair is the wrong man to have against you. If he sees you as a risk, you are out of the loop."

"Am I a risk?"

"Yes," Tomasa said. "For the moment, anyway. I'm afraid you won't have much freedom of movement in my country without his seal of approval."

"How do I get that?"

"He'll request a meeting with you. The arrangements will probably be made through Brognola. After that he will either pave the way for you, or put a roadblock in front of you. You just have to win his trust."

Bolan nodded. "Should *I* trust *him?*"

The BDU commander fell silent.

"And what about you?" Bolan asked. "Do you trust him?"

Tomasa thought long and hard before he gave St. Clair a qualified endorsement. "When I worked with him I trusted him with my life."

"When was that?"

"Back when Simon Liege was our adviser. He and Liege were very close at the time. Of course, St. Clair was close with most of the British SAS and SBS advisers. A man in his position had to be."

Reading between the lines, Bolan could see that the Belizean special forces man was in a tricky situation. They were hunting a man who had once been a close friend of St. Clair's. How hard would St. Clair try to find him? Or, worse, was it possible that St. Clair was collaborating with the DOA leader?

"Looks like we've got to update our intelligence," Bolan said. "We didn't even know St. Clair was still involved to this degree. Are there any other players I should know about?"

"Several," Tomasa said. "For example, there is a cartel figure in Belize City we may be able to exploit. He's not very happy with the idea of a permanent fighting force such as DOA. Especially if it is run by Simon Liege."

"Why's that?" Bolan asked. "Is there bad blood between them?"

"Gallons of it," Tomas said. "It stems from an incident when Liege was working with the Belize Defense Force. He and several of his British trainers were tipped off to a thousand bricks of cocaine that was being stored in Belize City, waiting for transit. They hit the place in the middle of the night and wasted the crew guarding it. The cocaine was never seen again. Supposedly, it was scattered into the ocean."

"The cartel chief doesn't think so?"

Tomasa shook his head. "And neither do I. Not anymore. But at the time Liege seemed beyond reproach. We know better now."

"Who is this cartel figure?"

"In time you'll learn everything you need to know," Tomasa promised. "My people are looking into all of Liege's connections. Old friends, old flames, people who love him and people who hate him. We will have plenty of targets to choose from."

"Provided I get St. Clair's seal of approval," Bolan said.

Tomasa nodded. "That's the way it is."

"However this thing works out," Bolan said, "I appreciate your help."

The commander stood and shook his hand. "And I yours," he said. "To be honest, no one I know would have gone after Sandor in such a direct manner. Even if St. Clair declares you persona non grata, you can still call on me."

"But what if he puts you on his enemies list?"

"Then I'll have to make a list of my own," Tomasa said. A dark light flashed in his eyes just before he turned and headed for the door. Bolan recognized the look. It was the look of a warrior who would choose his own battles. It was the same look that had always stared back at him from the mirror. If St. Clair stood in their way, they would run over him.

As he watched the Dragon Unit leader hurry across the sand toward the speedboat rocking in the rough water, he had a feeling he would see him again in the near future. Felix Tomasa wasn't a man to sit around and wait for the enemy to strike.

TWO HOURS AFTER his introduction to Tomasa, Bolan was jogging along the shoulder of the coastal road. The storm had passed, but the evening air was still cool. It was a night mean for running.

Now and then the soldier veered off from the road to avoid the occasional traffic that zipped by. He was on his third mile when he felt that he was being watched.

He glanced behind him and saw a black car coming down the road. From its current range it looked like the only person in the car was the driver.

Unlike the other cars that had passed, it was moving slowly, as if the driver were intentionally hanging back.

Bolan stopped jogging. He walked slowly along the road as if he were catching his breath. His hands were in the pockets of his windbreaker.

The car slowed to a crawl when it reached him.

There was a light whirring sound, and the automatic window rolled down.

"Pardon me, sir," the driver said. "But I'm looking for the road to Brooklyn, and I think I took a wrong turn—"

Bolan grinned. "Carvaggio!"

"In the flesh," the driver said, bringing the car to a complete stop.

Bolan approached the car and crouched to peer in through the window. "What the hell are you doing here?"

The former Mob hit man raised his eyebrows. "Good thing I'm not here to whack you," he said. "Otherwise you'd be dead by now."

"I wouldn't be too sure about that, guy," Bolan said. His right hand came out of his windbreaker pocket, the one that had been pointing at the car all along. It held the compact 9 mm Walther P-88.

Carvaggio cracked a smile, then nodded his approval at the weapon. "Glad to see you're still on your toes. Get in. I'll take you for a ride."

Bolan climbed into the late-model car. It was a Cadillac, of course, with all the trimmings. Even in Belize Carvaggio liked to travel in style. He shook hands with the man who helped him win one of his deadliest wars against the Mob, then clasped his shoulder. There weren't too many men that Bolan called friend, but this was one of them.

Bolan shook his head as Carvaggio wheeled the car back out onto the road. "I knew you were in-country," he said, "but I never expected to see you this close. What are you doing here?"

"Two things," Carvaggio said. "First, take a look in the back."

Bolan saw a travel blanket folded neatly on the seat.

"Under the blanket."

The soldier reached over and lifted the blanket, revealing the harness that held his Beretta.

"Greetings from Brognola," Carvaggio said. "I touched base with him in Belmopan."

"Thanks," Bolan said, picking up the precision-made piece that he'd come to rely upon. "What else?"

"Hmm?" Carvaggio said, keeping his eyes on the road as it went around a hairpin turn.

"You said there were two things that brought you here. What else?"

"Oh, yeah, that," he said, glancing at the Executioner. "I came here to kill you."

"What?"

"DOA sent me. They want me to find the man who killed their precious little colonel. I assumed that was you as soon as I heard about it."

Carvaggio filled him in on his chance to move up through the ranks of DOA. He also passed on some of the same intelligence he'd given to Brognola. Names, locations of the few DOA hideouts he knew about. Brognola was already tasking surveillance teams with watching the places.

After he digested the intel Bolan asked the question that had been on his mind ever since he heard that Carvaggio was with the DOA. "Can you get close to Liege?"

"Not yet. He fields a lot of troops, but it's a virtual army. Most of us never see him. He's got safehouses in Colombia, Peru, Mexico, Belize. Most of his soldiers work as bodyguards for the cartels until he sends them into action."

"No surprise there," Bolan said. "Liege is putting his people in position to do a hit on anyone who doesn't go along with his plans. That, or take over their territory for himself."

"That's the ultimate goal," Carvaggio agreed. "He's not powerful enough yet, but he's ruthless enough to get there."

"Unless we stop him."

"That's why I'm here," Carvaggio said. "Aside from taking you out."

They looked hard at each other, acknowledging something that lurked in the back of their minds ever since they first collided in the Judas operation. Who would prevail if it ever came down to a one-on-one situation?

The moment passed. Though in the distant past they were on opposite sides of the war, they were allies now.

"You have complete freedom of movement?" Bolan asked. "I thought Liege kept a tight rein on his people."

"He does," Carvaggio said. "When they're not on special ops. I have to check in now and then, but until I hear different you're my main assignment."

"Good," Bolan replied. "I'll need you close by my side in a day or two. I've got a meeting coming up with a guy named St. Clair, and I don't feel good about it. You know the name?"

Carvaggio shook his head. "No, but I'll see what I can find out."

"Do that," Bolan said. "In the meantime stay in touch with Brognola. He'll let you know when and where it's going down."

"Count on it."

"I am, Nick," Bolan said.

They drove around for another half hour, sharing intel and catching up with the paths they'd taken since last they met. Then Carvaggio drove back down to the long stretch of road where he first found Bolan.

"One more thing," Carvaggio said when he pulled over to the side of road.

"What?"

"You're a bit too easy to find out here."

"Yeah," Bolan said. "But only because Hal drew you a map. Besides, it's only temporary."

"So's life."

9

If there really was a shadow government in Belize, then Mack Bolan was breaking bread with the shadow governor himself, Alexander St. Clair.

Since his meeting with Felix Tomasa, Bolan had learned a lot more about the man who was sitting across the restaurant table from him.

St. Clair was a native born Belizean with a long and secret history. Former spook. Former statesman. Currently a retired adviser to most of the covert military and police units that were part of the Belize Defense Force. St. Clair held the keys to the covert kingdom, and if Bolan wanted more cooperation from the BDF this was the man to see.

For this night's meeting, St. Clair had selected a hotel-and-restaurant complex on the edge of the Serra rain forest just an hour's ride south from Belmopan.

It catered to eco-tours, mostly groups of well-off Americans and Europeans who came to the plush resort to stop and smell the orchids, snap a few shots of the tropical birds, and then sample some world-class cuisine.

The second-floor dining room was an air-conditioned observation post that looked out upon miles of sky-high treetops. It was like sitting inside a waterless fish tank, Bolan thought. Definitely not his idea of fun. He'd seen enough rain forests and jungles to last a lifetime.

But his host seemed to be enjoying himself, and he was the one who'd picked the crowded and costly spot. Dinner was uneventful until a little voice in Bolan's head told him all hell was about to break loose.

"We got two black hats checking out your car, Striker. They came out of the woods flanking the parking lot. They got camous and Hush Puppies."

Carvaggio's voice came loud and clear through the flesh-colored miniaturized earpiece Bolan wore for the meet and greet. Black hats, the Executioner thought. Carvaggio's way of saying two men from the other side were showing an unhealthy interest in the SUV and their owners. He only used the term for serious threats to life and limb. Hush Puppies meant they were carrying silenced side arms.

"Is something wrong, Mr. Belasko?"

The soldier studied the Belizean power broker sitting across the table from him. Gray hair, designer glasses, casually elegant suit that hid the extra weight he was carrying around. St. Clair looked more like a businessman than a veteran cloak-and-dagger man.

The rumors that he was in the pocket of the cartels couldn't be ignored. But so far they were just rumors. There was no guarantee he was bent. After all, every covert operator in Central America had some dealings with the opposition.

"I'd skip coffee if I were you," Bolan said.

St. Clair gave him a sideways glance, looking slightly perplexed and entirely innocent. That increased his odds of staying alive. No matter who he was, if he'd been involved in setting up Bolan, he would be the first to go.

"I'm afraid I don't quite understand."

Bolan leaned forward in a confidential manner. St. Clair followed suit a moment later, which made their private conversation that much clearer for the hidden mike beneath Bolan's shirt that was transmitting every word to Carvaggio.

"Things might get dangerous if we stick around much longer."

"For whom?"

"You're probably in the best position to answer that," Bolan replied.

"I still don't follow you."

"For your sake I hope that's true."

Bolan and St. Clair were supposed to be the only ones who knew about the meeting. St. Clair chose the location because it was sufficiently removed from the capital, reducing the chances they'd be seen by the wrong parties. Unless the spook had brought the wrong parties with him, Bolan thought. Had the man tipped off DOA? Or was he being followed?

"Right now there are two men checking out my car," Bolan said. "They've been watching it since you met me in the parking lot. You know anything about that?"

"Not a thing," St. Clair said, still wearing his mask of innocence. He was either very good at his tradecraft or else he really didn't know there were a couple of heavies outside in the darkness. "What do you make of it?"

"If they're not with you, two possibilities come to mind," Bolan said. "They're a couple of mechanics interested in a slightly damaged Land Rover..."

"Or?"

"They want to take one of us on a long unpleasant ride."

Carvaggio's voice came through his earpiece again. "Another car pulled in and parked right across from yours. Black SUV with a heavy mob inside. At least four men. Can't miss it. Looks just like a hearse. The first two guys came out of the woods, said something to the driver, and then went back into hiding."

Four more shooters, Bolan thought. More insurance for the hit and run. "A carload of triggermen just arrived. I suppose they're not yours?"

The Belizean man looked genuinely surprised. "No," he said, emphatically shaking his head. "Absolutely not."

"Looks like we're not going to leave here as quietly as we came," Bolan told him. "They've got to be DOA. Are you carrying?"

"Yes," St. Clair said. "Never could break the habit."

"Willing to use it?"

"If necessary," he stated, although the idea obviously had no appeal for him. "But it's been a while since I've been out in the field. I'll have to follow your lead."

"That's the plan," Bolan said.

"One thing before we go," St. Clair said. "How do you know anyone's out there?"

"I brought a friend with me," Bolan said. "He's keeping me posted as we speak."

"That wasn't part of the agreement," St. Clair said. "We were supposed to come alone."

"Want me to send him away?"

St. Clair shook his head. "Who is he?"

"Come on outside and I'll introduce you," the soldier said, pushing away from the table. "We'll go out the back way."

The Belizean fixer nodded. His calm manner impressed Bolan. He'd covered his shock from the rest of the guests, and outwardly he didn't seem frightened at all. He acted just like a man who'd been in these situations before. On both sides.

St. Clair opened a well-filled wallet and dropped enough U.S. dollars onto the table to cover a large dinner party and a generous tip. And maybe a bullet hole or two, Bolan thought.

On their way to the back of the restaurant they passed several couples lingering over dessert and strongly scented Belizean coffee. For a moment Bolan wondered what it would be like to be just like everyone else in the restaurant, enjoying a meal and thinking nothing about the endless covert wars that raged around them.

They pushed through the kitchen doors and stepped into the controlled chaos of cooks and waiters too busy to notice the strange duo walking past them.

But an officious little man in a white jacket took notice of them right away. He headed straight for St. Clair, raising his hand as if he were going to stop him. When he saw the cold distant look in Bolan's eyes the man in the white jacket looked at his raised hand as if it were suddenly possessed. He lowered his hand and backed away.

Bolan pushed through the rear door and stepped out onto a wide wooden deck with a steep set of stairs leading down into the darkness.

A warm gust of wind struck them. The air felt heavy, as if a storm were about to hit. A lead storm, Bolan thought. He drew the Beretta 93-R from the tearaway strap inside his jacket and scanned the shadowy curtain of forest.

"Let's do it," he said, more to Carvaggio than to the Belizean operative.

The wooden steps shuddered beneath them as they made their way down the back stairs, but the noise was covered by the thrumming of an air-conditioning unit and the night breeze hissing through the trees.

Bolan kept St. Clair ahead of him every step of the way. His trust in the man was growing somewhat, but he'd trust him a lot more if they walked away in one piece.

They inched toward the corner of the building and looked out at the horseshoe-shaped parking lot that was carved out of the forest. It was covered with crushed gravel and had only a single opening that formed a natural choke point. Anyone who tried to slip through it would have to pass a DOA gauntlet.

Bolan studied the black utility vehicle parked directly across from his Land Rover. It did look like a hearse, he thought. A lot of horsepower and even more firepower. There were four shapes inside. The undertakers.

There was no sign of the other two men.

"I'll circle around the Rover," Bolan said.

"What do you want me to do?" St. Clair asked.

"A suspicious man would tell you to step out into the open and see if you draw their fire."

St. Clair laughed. "Are you a suspicious man?"

"I'm getting over it," Bolan said. "Stay here until we need you, then come out firing." He pointed at the DOA hearse. "That's your target. Limit your killzone to the vehicle. Anything else out there might be us."

The Executioner slipped into the woods.

THE DOA TRIGGERMEN stayed hidden at the very edge of the rain forest, shrouded by a thick canopy of shadows. One on the left, one on the right, each with a clear line of fire at the Land Rover. They were merged with the darkness, leaning against thick tree trunks with tangles of vine draped around them like veils.

Their camous and military-style caps blended in with the dark green forest, making it almost impossible to see them from a distance. Only when they shifted position, impatiently willing the vigil to end, could they be seen.

Bolan drifted toward the man on the left.

Carvaggio moved in from the right.

They'd been gliding through the forest for several minutes in a light-footed rhythm that took advantage of the wind-driven trees hissing all around them.

Bolan came to a dead stop ten yards behind the DOA gunman and pointed the suppressed barrel of the Beretta at the man's shadowy torso. He would fire only as a last resort, knowing that the flash from the barrel could tip off the backup squad parked on the far side. He and Carvaggio decided the best way to do this was to get up close and personal.

The Executioner studied his would-be assassin, who was

hugging the tree and peering at the restaurant. The man was a good head taller than Bolan and as solid as the tree trunk that sheltered him. Even without the thick snout of his suppressed automatic weapon resting against the jagged bark, the DOA commando was formidable. The hardman definitely wasn't a novice.

But he was so intent on catching his targets coming out of the restaurant that he hadn't once looked behind him. The would-be assassin was mentally rehearsing his kill and, if not for Carvaggio's earlier warning, Bolan might be taking his last bow right now.

The Executioner could picture it happening in a flash... He and St. Clair walk down the front stairs of the restaurant, well fed and unsuspecting. Two men stroll out from the woods with their guns leveled and fire two shots each. Two dead men later the hitters calmly walk over to the hearse and drive away before anyone comes out of the restaurant. Or if there's time they throw the bodies in the back and no one even knows a hit's gone down.

Nice and clean.

But Bolan and Carvaggio didn't play nice.

The Executioner tapped the chest mike with the back of his hand, sending two clicks to Carvaggio.

Two answering clicks drummed in Bolan's ear. That meant Carvaggio was ready to strike.

Rather than rush forward and risk alerting his prey, Bolan walked straight toward the commando, a slow-motion arrow quietly homing in on the target. But the DOA gunner stiffened at the last second, sensing that death walked behind him.

He spun faster than seemed possible for a man of his girth, swinging his gun hand around in a deadly arc.

Bolan's rigid left palm chopped straight into the man's wrist and crushed it back against the tree. The impact snapped open his hand, and the suppressed Heckler & Koch pistol dropped nose down into the brush.

The man didn't waste any time trying to cry out or retreat. Instead he ducked his head like a battering ram and smashed his skull into Bolan's head.

Pain washed out nearly every thought in his head. Except for survival. Even as the blinding pain ricocheted through every nerve ending inside his skull, a dim part of Bolan's subconscious perceived the hardman's left hand pulling a blade from a sheath on his right side and slashing it toward the soldier's heart.

Bolan's right hand pistoned forward and pinned the man's meaty forearm against his chest, using the resistance to push himself back at the same time. It diverted the slash, but the blade sliced through his jacket and cut like a razor across his ribs.

The Executioner's left palm rocketed up into the heavy man's chin in a shotput motion that snapped his head back almost far enough to break his neck. But the muscles in the man's thick neck held firm. He was still standing, still a potential threat.

Bolan pivoted on his right hip and followed through with a spear hand into his adversary's exposed throat. His rock-hard fingertips cored the man's Adam's apple, then curled downward and grabbed the front of the hardman's shirt.

The gunner toppled forward, his eyes widening and staring at Bolan for a long second. Just long enough for the lights to go out forever. Now he was DOA for real.

Bolan guided the falling body into the woods and stretched him flat on his back. Then he went through his pockets. Nothing. No wallet, no coins. A nonentity in every sense of the word. Which meant that any ID and traveling money were probably stashed somewhere in the hearse.

Bolan took some quick breaths to pump oxygen into his racing blood to slow it. As the pain from the hammerhead strike subsided to an almost bearable level, he drifted off to the right, nosing through the brush until he saw a silhouette crouching over a fallen body.

It had to be Carvaggio. Otherwise the DOA assassin would have shouted a warning.

"Nick," he said. "You okay?"

The former hit man's winded response came immediately. "Physically, yeah. Mentally, no. He almost had me."

"Same here," Bolan said, feeling the stinging air on his bloodied rib cage as he stepped out into the open. "They're good, whoever they are."

Carvaggio glanced through the curtain of trees and nodded at the shining black vehicle across the lot. "You think the rest of the crew saw anything?"

"We're still alive," Bolan said. "And they're still in the hearse."

"Let's make sure they stay there."

The two warriors stripped the camou shirts and paramilitary caps from the DOA commandos. They slipped on the shirts and tilted the caps forward to shadow their faces, then stepped out into the open.

ALEXANDER ST. CLAIR tightened his grip on the trigger of the self-cocking automatic pistol. A minute ago he thought he'd detected some motion in the tree line directly behind Belasko's Land Rover.

His gut quivered and his heart felt like a lead weight, pounding much too fast. It'd been too long since he'd been in a situation like this. He didn't have the strength or the will for a pitched battle.

These days St. Clair's weapon of choice was a carefully chosen word, a whisper into the right ear. He was a puppet master, not a trigger puller. He couldn't remember the last time he went out shooting, let alone fighting.

Dear God above, he thought, when the two shapes came out from the trees. It's happening.

Their casual footsteps scuffed through the gravel as they crossed the parking lot toward the carload of gunmen, holding the sound-suppressed weapons by their sides.

AT FIRST St. Clair expected to see Belasko and his backup man. But when the pair walked into a pool of moonlight, he got a better look. They were both wearing camouflage shirts and military caps.

It was the ambushers, he thought.

The men in the SUV thought likewise—until they recognized that there was something a bit off about the DOA triggermen. They weren't the right size or the right shape.

"It's not them!" the driver shouted. "Shoot—"

He flicked on the headlights, temporarily blinding the two men and splaying their long shadows across the gravel.

The gunner on the passenger side dived halfway out the window and started shooting before he could acquire a target. He ended up strafing the sky with a full clip of 9 mm autofire.

Three 9 mm rounds answered him with loud thwacks that riddled his wrist and upper arms, spraying gouts of blood and shattered bone into the air. He flopped back into the front seat as his submachine gun pinwheeled to the gravel.

Despite the cold fear sweeping through him, St. Clair could no longer watch from his concealed area. He gripped the pistol with both hands and sidled around the corner. Then he followed the barrel of the weapon that seemed to tremor in his sweating palms.

BOLAN'S FIRST SHOTS eliminated the threat hanging from the passenger's window. He zagged to the left, jumping out of the way of the headlights that speared across the parking lot. He kept firing the submachine gun he'd taken from the

DOA commando, tracking from left to right across the windshield.

The headlights popped at the same time, shattered by a few well-placed rounds from Carvaggio's captured Heckler & Koch. He raked the windshield with his remaining rounds.

Several pockmarks spiderwebbed the bullet-resistant glass before it imploded and showered the occupants of the SUV with glass shards and whining lead.

Two barrel-flashes streaked from inside the shattered window as the fatally wounded driver punched a couple of last rounds into the darkness. They were reflex actions, and he was dead before the echo of his gun shots died down, lifeless hands draped across the steering wheel.

A clattering burst of autofire burned the air by Bolan's head just as his Heckler & Koch clicked empty. He dropped the captured weapon and rolled to the ground, ripping the Beretta from the tearaway holster beneath the camou shirt.

His peripheral vision caught movement at the rear of the SUV where a DOA gunner was crouching behind an open door. He was using it as a shield while his weapon sought out Bolan. Spears of flame shot from the barrel, and a spray of gravel chewed into the Executioner's leg.

Bolan rolled out of the way of another volley that drilled into the ground beside him. He triggered a 3-round burst in return, but the shots went wide.

His target jumped out of the open door and ran at Bolan with the barrel of the subgun spitting flame. The burning rounds closed in on him like a magnet.

Bolan zipped him with a burst in the chest, and the man's head exploded.

Magic bullets. The bizarre thought sprang into Bolan's mind as a halo of blood surrounded the falling gunman. He knew he'd got square in the chest, maybe the throat, but there was no way he took off the top of his skull.

Then he looked to his left and saw why the DOA hitter was missing part of his temple. St. Clair stood there with his gun extended, firing two more rounds into the man who almost got Bolan.

The gunman's body was already slumped against the SUV. The impact of the additional rounds inspired a graveyard dance as he bounced back from the SUV and his dead legs crumpled under him.

The old man still had it.

"Nice work," Bolan said, getting to his feet.

"Yeah," St. Clair said, looking quite surprised. All these years away from the trenches had made him wonder what he'd do if he was ever in combat again. And know he knew the answer. He'd do whatever he had to.

Bolan and St. Clair approached the SUV from the left and looked through the windows at the bloodied interior. Nothing moved inside.

"All dead," St. Clair said.

"All clear," Bolan shouted to Carvaggio, who was approaching from the other side.

Carvaggio flung open the driver's door, grabbed his collar and tossed him onto the ground.

They did a rapid search of the SUV, scooping up a handful of passports, money clips and area maps from inside the glove compartment. The seats in the rear compartment were folded down and covered with weaponry. Ammo cases, automatic pistols, submachine guns and grenades.

"All this for the two of us?" St. Clair asked.

Bolan shook his head. "I think we were just the first on the list," he said. "These guys were on a mission."

By now the windows of the restaurant were crowded with astonished spectators peering down into the parking lot. Their faces were pressed to the glass for a better look.

So far no one had dared to venture outside.

"Let's go," Bolan said.

"I wish we could," Carvaggio replied, sitting in the front wheel and gripping the steering wheel. He nodded at the narrow mouth of the parking lot where a long black vehicle had just cruised to a stop.

It sat there gleaming in the moonlight. It was a virtual twin of the one they were in right now.

The backup crew.

"Another battle wagon," Bolan said, watching the windows of the SUV roll down and gun barrels poke out. "Let's hit them before they scope out what happened."

"I guess I'm driving," Carvaggio said.

"We'll meet you there," Bolan told him. He scooped up a handful of weaponry and slipped out the side door farthest from the second-string of SUV gunners.

Carvaggio switched on the ignition and stomped the gas pedal. The glassless hearse lurched forward, kicking up dual sprays of gravel as it fishtailed toward the only possible exit.

The blockaders opened up when he was halfway there, streaming autofire through the trashed SUV. But it was too late. By then Carvaggio had the nose of the SUV heading on a straight track. He crouched below the steering wheel, locking it in position with a death grip.

Some bullets whined overhead and added a few more holes to the interior. Others clattered into the reinforced bumper and grille.

Then the shooting stopped and the screaming began. Carvaggio's two-ton battering ram broadsided the other SUV. Metal groaned and bones splintered as it caved in the front and rear doors as well as the DOA soldiers unlucky enough to be next to them.

The impact bounced Carvaggio back several feet. He stomped the pedal again and rocketed forward. The nose of the former hit man's vehicle tore into the battered SUV and pushed it back another twenty yards. It rolled over twice and settled onto its back like a helpless turtle—except for the stinging rounds of lead that spit out from the window.

One of the DOA soldiers had managed to regain his senses. He kept firing at Carvaggio's attack vehicle to provide cover for a dazed DOA trooper trying to crawl out through the dented window frame on the other side. The man dug the metal stock of his subgun into the ground, using it as a lever to pull himself out into the open. He came to a stop right at Bolan's feet. He looked up into the eyes of the Executioner and did a one-handed push-up while he tried to aim his weapon.

Bolan dropped him with a quick burst from the Beretta, then crouched and lobbed a grenade through the window.

The main force of the blast punched a hole up through the chassis. The side blasts disintegrated the remnants of the DOA force.

A moment later St. Clair raced his Mercedes out of the parking lot and slowed next to the smoking wreckage, pausing just long enough for Bolan and Carvaggio to jump in.

St. Clair sped down the two-lane road that led back to civilization, slowing only when they were a couple miles from the rain forest resort.

He shook his head and looked over at Bolan. "I'm sorry about this," he said.

"Sorry?" Bolan repeated. "We've got a lot to thank you for. You came in at the right time. If not, we might be the ones lying on the ground."

St. Clair nodded, savoring the knowledge that he hadn't lost his warrior's edge. "No," he said. "I'm sorry I haven't heeded the warnings coming my way. I thought all this talk of a cartel army was the same old propaganda the Americans and the British always fed my people. Just more excuses to increase their sphere of influence."

"Uncle Sam stretches the truth at times," Bolan acknowledged. "I've been told my share of red, white and blue lies."

Carvaggio shook his head and laughed. "Haven't we all?"

St. Clair slowed the Mercedes as they went through a series of sharp turns. He looked at Bolan, then at the rearview mirror reflection of the hard-faced man in the back seat. "From here on in, both of you have my full support. Field units, intelligence, anything I can do to help find the people responsible for this. I'll expect the same cooperation in return."

"Just as long as you know what you're in for," the Executioner said. "Sometimes you might have to ask your people to look the other way. Other times they might have to lead the way."

"It can be arranged," St. Clair said.

"Then you'll have our full cooperation," Bolan replied. "Logistics, matériel, intelligence. Whatever it takes. If we coordinate our operations, we'll cut the risk of running into any more fatal surprises like this one."

"Speaking of surprises," Carvaggio said. "Won't the police be surprised when they find your Land Rover in the lot?"

"Couldn't be helped," Bolan said. "The DOA was all over that vehicle. Might be booby-trapped. Not worth the chance of trying to move it."

"No worries," St. Clair said. "I'll make sure the right people take over the investigation. Is there anything special they'll find?"

Bolan shook his head. "Same as we found in the SUV. Fake ID, passport, some traveling money, a few untraceable weapons."

"They'll find a good home."

10

Miami, Florida

The flight from Belize City to Miami took a little over two hours, about the same amount of time it took to watch the "Today Show," which was exactly what Bolan and the other two passengers were doing when the Learjet began to make its descent.

Just before the television was automatically turned off by the onboard control system, Bolan heard the local weather report for the Miami area.

It was going to be hot.

Armed with that earth-shattering news, the soldier tilted his seat back and closed his eyes, savoring the cool hissing air that circulated through the cabin for the rest of the flight.

The Learjet landed smoothly at Miami International Airport and rolled down a runway to a private terminal that was maintained by the U.S. Customs Service.

An armored tank disguised as a limo was waiting for them just outside the terminal.

Brognola climbed into the front seat and immediately began talking with the driver, an old hand who'd been in on dozens of Brognola's operations. The driver had been familiarizing himself with all of the possible routes their target might follow when his private jet landed later that evening.

Bolan and Felix Tomasa climbed into the middle seat and

absorbed the firsthand intel from the driver as he led them out of the airport.

A half hour later they were driving by the first stop on the projected tour.

By the time their quarry arrived in Florida they would have a man posted at every step of the way. Edward Volos, the man identified by Tomasa as the key figure in the Belize City cartel, was coming to Miami. It was a trek he made to his home away from home at least twice a month.

Aside from his business interests, Volos had a long-term paramour stashed away in the city, which was the main reason for his frequent visits. It was the perfect place to hit him, a place where he considered himself far removed from the prying eyes of the DOA and the BDF, who had him under constant surveillance back in Belize.

But that surveillance had stretched a lot farther than usual. Tomasa's Dragon Unit team kept an eye on him from the moment he walked out of his walled mansion to the moment he boarded his private jet at Belize City.

Now it was up to the second team.

Each man had a part to play. Brognola handled the logistics and planning. Bolan handled the execution. And Tomasa would play the peacemaker. If there was anyone left to make peace with.

MACK BOLAN was sitting beneath a faded yellow awning at an open air café in Little Havana, sipping a potent cup of coffee when his shirt pocket started vibrating.

He grabbed the cellular phone, thumbed a button and said, "Go ahead."

It was Brognola.

"Volos is here," the head Fed said. "The watch team saw him fly into Miami International."

Bolan glanced at his watch. "Just like clockwork," he said into the phone.

"He always is, according to Felix," Brognola agreed. "Thank God for that. Let's get it in motion."

"Is everyone in place?"

"Stationary squads are watching every stop on the route," Brognola said. "Everyone else is on the move."

"I'm on my way," the soldier stated. He paid the modest dinner bill, then shielded his eyes as he stepped out into the bright light. It was early in the evening, and the Florida sun was still gleaming down on the city.

An omen of good things to come, he thought.

He headed for the customs van parked on the street. It came fully loaded with advanced communications gear, weaponry, GPS and a stereo system preset to the Miami radio stations.

Unfortunately, it was black with tinted windows and for the past hour had been soaking up the unbridled rays of the sun. A suffocating wave of heat spilled out as soon as he opened the driver's door.

Bolan rolled down the windows, turned on the air conditioner, and as the temperature eased down to a cool seventy degrees, he drove off through the narrow streets in the working-class district.

Tobacco shops, cafés, music stores and specialty grocery shops flanked both sides of the street, all bearing signs in Spanish. In some respects, he still felt as if he were in a different country.

By the time he left Little Havana's busy streets the sun was starting to fade and the streets were filling with locals and tourists ready to go out on the town. And Bolan was just getting ready to go to work.

The target had arrived. A target of opportunity who could become either an ally or a corpse.

The Executioner was ready either way.

In the console beside the driver's seat, which usually held CDs, car phones and beepers, was the harnessed Beretta along with a sound suppressor and a clip full of eighteen good reasons for Volos to listen to him.

EDWARD VOLOS looked more like a diplomat than the leader of a Belizean crime family. He was well dressed and had a premature touch of gray that streaked both sides of his otherwise dark black hair. Though he was slightly built, there was an air of command about him as he exited the upscale South Beach nightclub owned by one of his holding companies.

Two bodyguards followed a few feet behind Volos, scanning the street with casual but alert gazes. The dark complexioned security men spoke with cultured British accents. Both were veterans of the Belize Defense Force who'd trained under the guidance of the SAS and had the kind of sophisticated background that was ideal for security work. Unfortunately, they were providing security for someone the BDF considered an outlaw.

An armored Mercedes-Benz waited at the curb where a third bodyguard opened the rear door just as Volos approached.

It was all carefully choreographed and done with utmost respect, as if Volos were a statesman on his way to conduct affairs of great import, although his most pressing affair involved the red-haired model he'd billeted in a gated mansion. She'd done commercials, she'd done print ads, but most importantly, she'd done Volos when he was at a particularly low point in his marriage. A walking, talking love doll, she'd restored the virility he thought he'd lost forever. Such a gift had to be repaid in kind.

That's why she became one of the wealthiest models in Miami, and one who never had to model again.

The Mercedes drove off slowly into the night, with Edward Volos the unknowing leader of a covert parade.

THE EXECUTIONER kept the black van several car lengths behind the Mercedes, falling back now and then to let some of the other chase cars move in.

There was little chance of losing Volos.

The intelligence Tomasa provided on the cartel chief was exact. Volos was a creature of habit whenever he visited Miami, and he was religiously following his itinerary, just like stations of the cross.

Fittings with a tailor, brief meetings with upper-echelon business associates in their private homes, private dinner at his club. Next on the menu was Melody Prime, the model formerly known as Karen before she took the advice of her agent and changed her name. She also changed her nose, her lips and her breasts so they conformed to the required specs for a Miami model.

After Bolan followed the car for another twenty minutes the Mercedes' brake lights came on. The vehicle turned onto a private road that cut through neatly manicured trees and led up to a gated paradise.

Bolan drove past the turnoff and pulled over to the side of the road. He drove the car another twenty yards on the shoulder, then killed the lights.

The soldier strapped on the Beretta's harness and stepped out of the van, carefully closing the door behind him. He kept the engine running in case one of Brognola's operatives had to move it in a hurry. This section of road had become an instant parking lot.

Unmarked cars lined both sides of the road. Some were wheeling around in three-point turns so their front ends were facing the distant driveway the Mercedes just entered. Several other cars continued ahead to set up roadblocks.

Volos had come here for some long needed privacy. Brognola's team was going to make sure that he got it.

Bolan joined the clandestine procession that was quietly

heading on foot for the Spanish modern home, a high-walled villa with electronically controlled gates.

The Mercedes had come to a stop several yards before the gate. The driver's left hand held a remote unit out the window and was aiming it at the control box mounted on the stone column.

Click.

Nothing happened.

He clicked the device again and swore under his breath. He angrily repeated the maneuver several times.

The four other men in the Mercedes were suddenly apprehensive. They looked out the window but saw nothing.

"No use," the driver said. "It's not working. Circuit must be damaged. Or she changed the code somehow."

"Maybe," Volos said. "Maybe it's something else." He took out his cellular phone and tapped the speed-dial button with Prime's number. It was a number she gave out to no one else.

He got a busy signal. The monotonous sound triggered an alarm deep inside of him. There could be harmless explanations for the failure of the gate *and* the phone. But coming one after the other, they were too coincidental to ignore. "Get us out of here," Volos ordered.

The driver glanced at the side mirror, about to back up, when he caught a glimpse of something moving. Several dark shapes were swarming out from the trees.

Before he could say a word something sharp impaled itself into his neck. He tried to swat it away with a furious swipe of his hand. His palm made a slapping sound on contact with his skin, loud enough to draw the attention of the others. Two more stinging barbs pierced the back of his hand.

A split second later the driver fell back into the car and tried to open his mouth, but it felt as if his blood were freezing inside of him and his jaw was locking up. The crystallizing sensation raced through his body and roared up to his brain.

His head plunked forward until his chin hit his breastbone.

"Get out of the car!" Volos shouted. "Everybody out—"

The bodyguard in the front passenger side was already leaping out of the door, his hand reaching under his jacket for his weapon. He spun, a towering figure with his hand stuck in his jacket. The only thing that could move were his eyes as they searched the darkness for his assailants.

Several other sharp projectiles zipped through the night, coming so fast they sounded like echoes of one another. They came from all directions, striking the bodyguard several times. The big man's knees folded beneath him.

The two other bodyguards received the same treatment, barely making it out of the doors before they were hit with the same type of projectiles.

Two customs vans raced up the driveway and formed a blockade behind the Mercedes.

The squadron of black-clad shapes that took out the bodyguards quickly moved forward and formed a cordon around the Mercedes. They trained their electrically powered silent dart guns through the open doors at the sole remaining passenger.

Each man carried an automatic submachine gun as backup in case the dart guns, officially known as microbioinoculators failed to do their job. The compact guns fired needle-shaped projectiles that flooded the bloodstream with a ketamine-based compound.

The concoction was the result of years of trial and error by CIA alchemists searching for the perfect truth serum. They accidentally discovered the perfect knockout drug. It immediately rendered the subject unconscious and left behind a headache along with amnesia.

Bolan stepped over one of the ketamine-dosed bodyguards and introduced himself to Volos by nosing the suppressed barrel of the Beretta into the open door.

The cartel leader didn't make a single move. Considering the ambush that had just taken away his protection, the spotlights shining on him from the back of the car, and the weapon pointed at his head, he remained fairly calm for a man in his position.

"I don't carry a weapon," Volos said, looking at the hard-eyed man wielding the Beretta.

"So I heard," Bolan said. "But there's always a first time. Step outside so we can make sure."

Volos glanced at the commandos hauling away the prone bodies of his men. "There was no need to kill my men."

Bolan jerked his head toward the bodyguards. "They're not dead," he said. "Right now the worst they're facing is a memory gap and one hell of a hangover. We know they're good soldiers—we didn't want to give them a chance to prove it."

The Executioner saw that Volos wasn't all that surprised. As if he knew the score and had nothing to fear from the man in black. Not good, Bolan thought. He wanted him on edge.

"We also wanted to show you how easy they can be eliminated when the time comes," Bolan said.

Volos nodded. He stepped out of the car and was quickly searched by one of the commandos. "Now what?"

"Now we talk," Bolan said. "This way," he said. He motioned the Beretta back down the driveway. Three of the commandos from Brognola's team followed along behind.

Others stood along the side of the driveway watching their progress.

Bolan didn't need that kind of protection for a single prisoner. Tactically, it was overkill. Psychologically, it was just another weapon in the arsenal. He wanted Volos to have a glimpse of the force that could be massed against him.

As they walked down the driveway, Volos glanced back at the house, aware that not only had his night been ruined, but possibly his life. After all, he was in a strange land surrounding by heavily armed men who held his fate in their hands. Still, he couldn't help thinking of the main reason for his visit. "What about Melody?" he said. "She'll be wondering what happened to us."

"No, she won't," Bolan said. "She'll be sleeping it off. Just like the others."

"You went after her, too?" Volos looked shocked. "She's got nothing to do with this."

"Try consorting with the enemy," Bolan said. "Or conspiracy to traffic drugs. Money laundering. Take your pick."

"But I am an innocent man," Volos protested. "I've been convicted of nothing in your country."

"Second part of that statement's right. But you're hardly innocent. Before you cry any tears, let me tell you some of the things we know. You stash a lot more than sugar in that house." Bolan nodded at the expansive villa behind the gates. The grounds behind the villa opened onto a private landing on the inland waterway. "We know it's occasionally used as a transshipment point for your Miami operation. And the cash that's flowing in and out of Melody's accounts are a bit rich for a girl with no income."

"You have no proof that will hold up in court," he said.

Bolan gave him a hard stare. "I usually settle these things out of court," he growled. "But even if we decided to go that route, we've got enough to hang you."

"Impossible," Volos said.

"Nothing's impossible with the technology we've got," Bolan told him. "Right now an army of accountants is sifting through your bank records and turning up some intriguing transactions. So far they found a half dozen front companies that make substantial donations to political figures and military officers with cartel connections. We've also got surveillance footage of your operations. Here and in Belize City.''

Volos shook his head, realizing the scope of the nightmare that he'd just walked into. ''What have I done to deserve this kind of attention?''

''You got in the way of DOA,'' Bolan said. ''That can help you or hurt you.''

''DOA brings no good to anyone connected to it,'' Volos said, beginning to catch a glimpse of the light at the end of the tunnel. It was faint. If it involved DOA, there was always a chance he could get buried in that tunnel and never see daylight again. ''What is it you want from me?''

''Come and hear our terms.''

When they reached the end of the driveway Bolan saw Hal Brognola just as he was climbing into the open side door of his customs van. The driver slid the door shut, then nodded. They were ready.

''This way,'' Bolan said, noticing Volos's appraising look as they passed the gauntlet of cars parked up and down the road. Covert operatives in Kevlar vests stood by their cars and impassively watched the cartel man pass.

''What are they all doing here?''

''At the moment they're protecting your life.''

''A novel experience,'' Volos said.

Bolan shrugged. ''Their orders are subject to change.'' He led Volos around to the other side of the van, yanked the sliding door open and ushered him inside the mobile command post. When they took the two remaining seats, Bolan closed the door behind him and sealed them into the air-conditioned and soundproof cabin.

The driver swung onto the road, ignoring his passengers.

The hollowed interior had four comfortable contour seats bolted into each corner. Positioned between the seats was a low flat table with Brognola's shoes resting upon it. He was sitting in the left rear corner, studying Volos with his best hatchet man face. It was the face of a man who could signal thumbs-up or thumbs-down on another man's life.

In the other corner was a face that was familiar to Volos. Felix Tomasa, the Belizean commander of the Dragon Unit. He nodded slightly at the cartel man.

Volos stared at the other man, squinting as if he couldn't believe his eyes. "Felix," he said, glad to see someone from his own country. Though they were on opposite sides, he knew that Tomasa was a man of his word. "You're keeping strange company these days."

"Good company," Tomasa said. "Can you say the same?"

"I can't really say anything. Until I know who I'm dealing with." He turned to Brognola, aware that he was the one running the show.

"I'm speaking for Uncle Sam," Brognola said. "I have the authority to keep you locked away forever or let you go back to Belize and deal with matters on your own."

The head Fed picked up a remote-control device and turned on the video screen that was built into the console behind the front seats.

Several different shots of the cartel boss appeared on the monitor. Volos standing outside his home, walking through the sculptured maze of his garden, speaking with confederates in Belize City. The next series of shots showed surveillance photos of his home in the capital and his retreat on the Caribbean coast. Blowups of license plates on the cars of his bodyguards. The final series of close-ups showed lists of his associates, phone numbers, bank accounts. The cornerstone of his empire.

"Get the picture?" Brognola asked.

"Yes. You're threatening me."

"No," Brognola said. "I'm showing you what you have

to lose. We have no personal vendetta with you. We're just taking precautions. Unless you join us, sooner or later Simon Liege will own everything on that screen. All those sites will become potential targets where we can hit him. We can hit him after he comes for you or before. It's up to you." He turned off the video.

"What happens if I say no? Do you tell everyone I'm cooperating with you and feed me to the sharks?"

Brognola shook his head. "That's why we arranged this…conference up here rather than on your home ground. Felix knows the situation down there. With everyone trying to keep tabs on each other, he thought this was the best way to do it. No one knows about it but us."

"And my men."

"Do you trust them?"

"Yes."

"Sounds like you've got nothing to worry about."

The cartel man nodded and sat back in his chair, mulling over his options as the customs van drove back to Miami. Outwardly he didn't reveal any fear. But he was a realist who knew when the end of the road was in sight.

Volos was a second generation cartel man, brought up to inherit the reins from his father. It came much sooner than anticipated thanks to a competitor's bullet.

Volos took over the Belize City cartel and ran it like a business. His first order of business was sending his men after the man who killed his father. After establishing that he wasn't to be trifled with, Volos quietly went about diversifying his empire, playing the game smart enough to make it to his early middle age.

Now he was facing an unintended retirement.

"What is the offer?" Volos asked.

"We need an insider who can lure DOA into the open," Brognola said. "Or point us in the right direction so we can find him."

"Liege has made overtures," the cartel chief admitted. "He wants me to become part of his unstoppable force. A Pan-American alliance, he calls it. DOA, a boundaryless city-state that recognizes no law but its own. But Liege is a cautious man. So far he's only worked through intermediaries. I doubt he'll accept an invitation to a dinner party."

"Is there any other way you can lead us to him?"

"Perhaps," Volos said. "But I still haven't heard the rest of the offer. If I cooperate, does that mean you overlook my enterprises?"

Bolan leaned forward. "We're not in the drug business," he said.

Volos acted surprised. "No? What about the riches that poured into Honduras and Costa Rica when your country based the Contras there? Guns in, drugs out. Same people, same planes. Everyone knew it, particularly your intelligence services."

Volos looked from face to face. This was his test to see how credible they were. Every man in the mobile conference room knew there was a lot of truth to what he said. The CIA looked the other way too many times during the Contra days. They hired pilots who'd been in and out of jail for drug trafficking. They used cargo planes that were owned by cartels. Many of the professional soldiers recruited into the Contra armies were known traffickers, bag men and murderers.

"I'm not going to sit here and get a lecture on right and wrong from a drug dealer," Bolan said. "It happened. But it was a mistake then and it's a mistake now. No one's getting a free ride anymore. Not on my watch."

Volos raised his eyebrows and looked over at Brognola. "Does he speak for you in this matter?"

"Yes, he does," Brognola answered.

"Then what do I get for helping you?"

"A chance to get out of the business while you still can,"

Brognola said. "Keep the fortune you made and start a clean slate."

"I can do that with or without you."

"True," Brognola said. "But how long will you live without us? DOA won't let you stay on the sidelines. You'll have to choose sides."

Volos exhaled. "I chose sides some time ago. Ever since Liege betrayed me."

"We know about the incident," Brognola said. "We figured you'd want to even the score."

"You figured right, gentleman," Volos stated. "Let's talk."

By the time the customs van reached Miami International Airport, Volos had given them several possible leads to Simon Liege. The most promising was a place near Belize's western border, a sweet leaf plantation near some ruins that Liege had taken over from Guatemalan rebels.

It had been a substantial operation at the time, producing planeloads of cannabis once the harvesting was done. Knowing Liege, he had expanded it into an even larger operation by now.

The site was perfect for DOA. It was located on a prime dope corridor that led right up to Mexico. Rain forest covered much of the area and provided refuge for an underground army that could live in the brush.

There were also several rivers throughout the area, giving plenty of ways to get in and out of there fast.

The van carrying Volos brought him right to the hangar where his private plane was kept.

Two other vans pulled alongside it. One of them contained several commandos who opened up the sliding doors of the remaining van. They quickly dragged out their unconscious cargo and deftly carried the slumbering bodyguards onto the plane.

Volos was the last one onboard, shaking his head as he

walked by the seats where his silent bodyguards lay, dead to the world.

They were his best soldiers, Volos thought, as the plane left the hangar and rolled down the runway. His very best. And they were handled as if they were green recruits. There was no doubt in his mind anymore. He'd joined the right team.

11

Cayo District, Belize

The Panther airboat skipped like a stone across the muddy brown river, boosted by a caged aircraft propeller with a 350-horsepower V-8 engine and two forty-gallon tanks.

Felix Tomasa sat propped up in the contoured front seat with his Colt AR-15 assault rifle pointing sky high. He was as still as a masthead, except for his feet vibrating from the thrumming of the smooth-bottomed boat that plowed through the water at fifty miles an hour. The Dragon Unit leader was in his element, calmly absorbing the bumps and jolts of the river.

The boat and the weaponry were part of the fleet provided to the Belize National Police by their partners in U.S. Customs. It was a natural fit. The BNP riverine unit was composed of men who'd practically grown up in the rough waters off the Belizean coast or on the rivers that carved up the interior. With the ability of the flat-bottomed airboats to skim over shallow water, there were few areas in Belize the special teams couldn't reach.

Behind the commander sat a second gunner. He was riding low on a floor-mounted side seat that let him train his automatic weapon on the left bank. He had the safety on and expected no trouble on this stretch of the river, but long years of training kept him ready for anything that could be thrown at him.

The pilot worked the steering lever with one hand, keeping his other hand free for the muzzle-up .357 Smith & Wesson pistol in his spring-loaded shoulder holster. Like the others, he was relaxed but ready.

All three of them had spent considerable time as Belizean "shipriders," special operatives who accompanied U.S. Customs helicopters, patrol boats or oceangoing interceptors on drug busts in Belizean territory. The joint patrols scoured sea and land for the growing number of traffickers who found the largely unsettled regions of Belize a paradise for their trade. It would be a paradise lost unless they stopped them.

The problem was finding them. Belize was about the size of Massachusetts but had a population only slightly over two hundred thousand. Most of the people lived near the coast or in the handful of inland cities. That left plenty of undiscovered land to get lost in, and the traffickers took full advantage of the situation.

In the early days the police were unprepared to deal with the new breed of trafficker. But after making countless busts with the customs agents, they learned the tricks of the trade and added a few of their own.

Now the BNP Dragon Unit was the heart of the counter drug operation. When they weren't working with customs the special boat teams patrolled the rivers that were the lifeblood of the small fishing villages scattered throughout the interior. Along with maintaining stability in the frontier regions and developing relationships with the locals, they responded to tips like the one that had been provided by Edward Volos.

The claims of the most recent convert to the cause proved to be right on target. While there were many small-time native traffickers working in the western forest regions near Guatemala, the large-scale operations were controlled by foreigners like Simon Liege. He knew more about this part of the country than people who had lived there all of their lives. Liege also had the connections to grow, harvest, package and ship the cannabis out of the country.

Marijuana farms provided a reliable and profitable backup to the cocaine trade. It was like a bank, always there to provide cash reserve in emergencies. And a special forces veteran with Liege's skills knew how to keep it hidden.

Until now.

The airboat armada knew exactly where to find the doper plantation. They weren't going in blind, and they weren't going in alone. Airborne units were circling around the region, flying undetected at high altitude until the time came for them to move in.

Now and then Tomasa caught movement from the thick green shrouds of forest that draped over the banks of the rivers.

Ferns slashing the air.

Faces peering out from cover, then vanishing. Could be fishermen, he thought. Could be hunters.

It wasn't unusual for the riverside inhabitants to see the Panther airboats plying the waters of western Belize. Nor was it unusual for them to duck back out of sight. A lot of them liked to keep to themselves. And they liked to keep civilization at bay.

To them it had to have seemed as if they were being invaded by a regular navy. The boat squadron seldom traveled in large groups, typically no more than three boats with five-man crews. But this day they had ten of the high-speed crafts with them. Some boats had three-man crews. Others had five.

It was a considerable force. For the task ahead of them it had to be. From the intelligence gathered by the American recon crafts, it was obvious that a large group was present in the area.

The jungle-based group could be made up of hard-core

doper crews, Guatemalan guerrillas cultivating crops from across the border, or DOA soldiers.

There was no way of knowing yet.

But whoever it was, they were in for a surprise.

The commander scanned both sides of the river, using his peripheral vision to take in the blurring green countryside. In the back of his mind was the thought of a DOA ambush.

Emerald Caye cost them. So did the firefight at the restaurant. The DOA had obviously been shadowing Alexander St. Clair to see which side he was on. They'd found out the hard way, and now they were looking to get back at someone. Who better than the Dragon Unit? If the DOA mercs took on the Belizean special forces and won, it would make them look unstoppable.

Tomasa found his thoughts drifting back to the meeting they had in Miami with Volos. All things considered, Volos seemed calm for a man with his back up against the wall. Though he couldn't have known where or when, he'd almost seemed to be expecting an approach by Brognola's team. What if Liege had reached Volos before Brognola did? What if the two of them had planned this all along, the cartel boss feigning cooperation with Brognola only to send them into a DOA ambush...

No, he thought. That would mean Volos would have to go underground like Liege. Tomasa figured Volos had become too accustomed to the high life for that. He was a long-distance soldier, someone who worked behind the scenes instead of putting himself on the front line.

Tomasa knew it was just his nerves kicking in, the way they always did before he went into a combat zone. He didn't know if it was going to be a routine patrol or an all-out war.

That's why the ten airboats were spread out in a long string on the river. They couldn't be taken all at once if the enemy was waiting for them.

The airboat suddenly dropped speed as they neared the backwater village that was the closest settlement to the marijuana farm. Tomasa's pilot let up on the gas pedal even more, then levered the rudders toward a narrow channel.

The aluminum-hulled Panther skimmed across a muddy strip of water that was flanked on both sides by houses on stilts. Thatched roofs, plywood walls, easily built homes that were just as easily blown down by the storms that swept through the area.

Motorboats and canoes lined the banks. The water was extremely shallow, but like most of the boats that were tied up along the tributary, the airboat could easily navigate through it.

Two other airboats passed by the tributary. Another one followed the lead vessel just into the mouth of the channel and turned with the nose facing the river.

The lead pilot drifted up to a small dock, slowing inch by inch until the aluminum bow just barely touched the ramshackle berth. It slid against the wood and came to a soundless stop.

A dirt trail led from the dock up to the largest house in the village. It was a barn-shaped structure that was on stilts like the other houses, but it looked considerably more substantial. This was the community gathering place and the home of the unofficial mayor, a man in his seventies who'd been the man in charge back when Belize was still known as British Honduras.

By the time Tomasa jumped onto the dock, the mayor had come out of his house and was heading for the dock in long rapid strides. His name was Uxpenk Tumal, otherwise known as Grandfather to everyone in the riverside community.

Tumal had the muscle tone of someone decades younger. He wore a white cotton short-sleeved shirt and drawstring pants. His forearms were heavily veined, dark blue tributaries pumping blood through slabs of sinewy muscle. There was a long knife sheathed at his side, and he had a glint in his eye that said he was ready for anything. The only real sign of age was in his gleaming dome. He was practically bald except for the silvery tufts on the side of his head.

A half dozen children ran after him as he warmly greeted Tomasa.

The Dragon Unit leader climbed out of the airboat and into the maelstrom of village kids who chattered endlessly at him while they tugged at his jungle green fatigues and asked for candy and cigarettes.

"Sorry," Tomasa told them. "We had no room for supplies on this trip."

The tallest one of them pointed at the packages that lay in the bottom of the boat and laughed at Tomasa for not seeing them.

"You're right," the commander said. "I almost forgot." He nodded at the gunner, who grinned and started stacking several boxes onto the deck. Medicine, first-aid kits, soda and cigarettes. All the things that were scarce in the frontier. Customary gifts for the local chief.

The old mayor clapped his hands and sent the children off to his home, each of them carrying one of the packages.

Unlike the children who were eager to see the police officers, Tomasa noticed some of the other villagers drifting away. They were clearly uneasy at the presence of the special boat team.

For the first ten minutes Tomasa sat on the mayor's shaded porch and made small talk while they smoked cigarettes and drank tea. Finally, Tumal signaled that it was time to talk. He pinched the burning end of the cigarette between his callused thumb and forefinger and carefully set it on the table beside him. "Now," he said. "What brings you here? And why so many of you."

"The farm."

"Farm?" Tumal said, looking toward the jungle at the end of the clearing. "The jungle is our farm."

The Dragon Unit leader laughed. He knew what the old man meant. Palms, nuts, pineapples, bananas, sap. Just about all of their essentials could be easily harvested from the jungle. The rest of their diet was made up of what they could hunt, trap or fish.

Tomasa shook his head. "I'm talking about the marijuana farm. About five miles upriver."

"Ah," the mayor said. "I see."

"So you know about it."

"We know everything that goes on here."

"Do you know who runs this farm?"

"No," Tumal replied. "Not by name. But it is good you are here." He told Tomasa about the new arrivals to the farm. Unlike the original group who were mostly transplanted hippies and drifters, this crew had a harder edge to them. Thuggish men who always carried arms with them. "They bring trouble wherever they go," he said.

"What kind of trouble?"

"There have been incidents," the old man said. "The women in our village don't feel safe. The men have been threatened. So far no one has been hurt. On our side." He smiled.

Tomasa could picture the old frontiersman manhandling any hard cases who strayed into his village. Despite their serene way of life, the villagers had grown up in hard surroundings. They were skilled with bows, shotguns and hunting rifles. Weapons were an everyday tool for them, and they didn't scare easily.

"Why didn't you come to us earlier?" Tomasa asked.

The mayor raised his hands as if it were a matter for the gods to decide. "If we brought you here, they would punish us. Retribution. But if you discover them yourselves, there is nothing they can do."

Tomasa was silent. He understood the old man's logic, but the old man didn't yet understand what they were up against.

"Is there?" the mayor asked.

Tomasa thought about DOA and how quick they were to slaughter anyone who stood in their way. If the police went in and destroyed their operation, they would seek vengeance. The villagers would have to be moved out of the area, which he doubted was possible. This was their land, and they weren't the type who moved for anyone. The other choice was for the Dragon Unit and the airborne strike force to wipe out the DOA presence entirely.

He spoke with the village headman a while longer, telling him to get his people ready in case they had to be evacuated.

"Why?"

"These people may be worse than you know," he said. "If it's the ones we're looking for, they are here to make war."

"Against who?"

"Against everyone who isn't on their side," the Dragon Unit commander said. "Their name is DOA, and their leader is Simon Liege." He described Liege, the lean leader of the mercs.

"No," Tumal said. "He's not with them. Or he hasn't shown himself. But whoever the newcomers are, they're a different breed. The first group that worked the farm wanted to learn our ways. Imagine, all those rich foreigners hiking across the world and coming to our backyard. Hoping to live in the trees and harvest their sweet leaf."

Tomasa understood the man's philosophy. To him, cultivating marijuana fields was a natural occupation. Just another cash crop that came from the earth. It made no difference to him what they grew there until they became a threat to their peaceful way of life. The first breed of dopers hadn't bothered them at all. But the hard-core traffickers were a different story. Tumal and his people just wanted to be left alone.

"We both know how dangerous these people can," Tomasa said. "Will you let us help you?"

The old man nodded. "As much as possible," he said. "I don't think my people will want to move."

"What will they do?"

"Fight, of course," Tumal said. "We were here before anyone else. We will be here after they are gone."

"What about your women and children?" Tomasa asked. "Will they be expected to fight too?"

The old man sighed. "Perhaps it's best for them to go away for a while. Can you guarantee their safety?"

"Only if they come downriver with us on our return trip," Tomasa said. "Get them ready as soon as you can. If there's any trouble, it's going to start now."

He spent several more minutes talking with the village headman to glean whatever intelligence he could about the unwelcome and heavily armed neighbors who had camped out in the jungle. It didn't add much to what he already knew, but it confirmed that the mayor was playing straight with him. The old man's description of the marijuana fields dovetailed with the briefings he and his men received.

The mayor even drafted a rough map of the terrain, smoothing a sheet of paper on the porch table and using a quill pen to sketch out the terrain. Though it was primitively drawn and derived solely from his travels on the ground, it was a good match with the overhead recon shots that Brognola's team had provided them.

Tomasa thoroughly looked over the map before setting it back down on the table. The mayor snatched up the map and crumpled it in his fist. Then he held it over the ashtray and lit one of the ragged corners.

"Destroying the evidence?" Tomasa asked, watching the smoke and flame consume the map.

"No," the mayor said, permitting a slim smile to show on his weathered face. "It is a ritual. You help us, we will help you." He held on to the burning paper until it began to singe his callused hand. It dropped into the ashtray and broke into a bed of burned ashes.

Tumal passed his hand over the ashes once, twice, as if he were sealing the fate of the trespassers on the map.

"Now you can go."

He left with the mayor's blessing. Tomasa would welcome all the help he could get.

TOMASA'S AIRBOAT caught up with the rest of the special boat squadron as the Dragon Unit Panthers knifed through the water. Behind each boat trailed a long furrow of churning foam, whipped by the engine propeller that pushed it across the water like a giant fan.

His pilot floored the pedal and rocketed past the others before swerving into the lead position.

The bottoms of the aluminum boats shuddered when they hit a patch of rough water, rattling their bones and jarring their teeth, but the men of the Dragon Unit were used to it.

Tomasa glanced up at the sky. He couldn't see anything, but he knew the fleet of special operations aircraft were nearby.

An AC-130 Spectre gunship and an MC-130 Combat Talon had taken off from Ladyville Airport, the main base for joint U.S. and Belizean training operations and drug interdiction missions. It was located a few miles up the coast from Belize City, less than sixty miles from the western border. Each plane had a Belize Defense Force officer riding along with the U.S. crew.

The special operations planes had a lot of firepower and advanced surveillance systems, adding their recon capacity to the other aircraft that had been scouting the area ever since Volos had provided them with leads to the ganja farm.

A squadron of MH-53 Pave Low and Sikorsky Seaguard helicopters was en route from the airport at Belmopan, carrying Brognola's special operations group and their BDF counterparts.

Several U.S. Customs planes were also in the air, including two Cessna 206s and a Cessna 404 Titan that was outfitted with surveillance gear and extra fuel tanks. The additional fuel tanks could keep the relatively small plane aloft for up to sixteen hours at a time, allowing it to unobtrusively track smugglers wherever the trail led them.

The Cessnas were the key to the entire mission. Each plane was equipped with latest generation dope detector cameras that used hyperspectral optical technology to locate marijuana fields. Each camera was programmed with the unique color signatures of cannabis plants. During overflights of suspect territory, the camera scanned the entire color spectrum, filtering out surrounding vegetation and immediately registering hits on targets that matched the cannabis specs.

So far the dope detector cameras had identified three large plots sprinkled through the jungle, containing approximately nine thousand plants that ranged from six to ten feet tall.

At minimum, each plant was worth three thousand dollars. If all of it made it to the street market, the pot farmers would get a yield of up to twenty-seven million dollars.

Not a bad cash crop, Tomasa thought. Enough to bankroll a small army. Enough to kill for if they were DOA.

When they were a half mile away from the targeted dope zone, Tomasa signaled the pilot to slow down and move in toward the closest shore. As the airboat neared a bend in the river the commander flipped open the sat-com gear that connected him to Brognola's airborne SOG group. A moment later he spoke to the man he knew by name as Michael Belasko. "We're going in," he said.

The lead airboat rounded the bend and immediately nosed

toward the left bank, drifting right up to the river's edge. When the vessel was a few yards from shore Tomasa gripped the side of the boat for balance and jumped into the water. He held his Colt rifle overhead as the mucky river bottom sucked at his high rubber-soled jungle boots. He sunk deeper into the muck with each step as he scrambled through the thigh-high water to the jagged bank. At the water's edge he grabbed a handful of vines and pulled himself up onto the bank.

His gunner sloshed through the water a few feet behind him and tossed his gear up onto the shore.

The pilot cruised to the other side of the river and nestled the airboat under the drooping eaves of a cluster of trees that slanted out over the water. From the leafy green harbor he could see a wide stretch of the opposite bank and could jet to any point he was needed.

One by one the other boats leapfrogged past Tomasa's position, spreading out along the riverbank to drop off the Dragon Unit commandos and their gear. Weapons, radios and ropes.

Each man spread out about twenty yards from each other, about the approximate amount of visibility they could expect once they entered this sector of dense green jungle.

When the last man climbed up to the bank Tomasa signaled them to move in. They began filtering into the forest, stepping slowly through the thick underbrush with their weapons pointing the way.

The Dragon Unit carried a variety of arms that ranged from shotguns to sleek wooden crossbows that were specially designed for jungle fighting. They could fire up to five bolts at a time, and their wooden frames were camouflaged to blend in with the surrounding jungle.

For automatic weapons most of them carried a CAR-15 or a 7.62 mm Belgian FAL. The lightweight FAL weapons were ideal for jungle conditions, dependable in the extremely wet climate and versatile enough to be used as a streamlined grenade launcher.

Tomasa held a CAR-15 fitted with a double magazine at his side, sweeping the barrel slowly from side to side to cover his field of fire. He felt comfortable with the weapon due to his extensive training with the U.S. Customs special ops, who favored it for close-quarters combat.

The ground team moved in tandem, checking the zones in front of them and keeping the others in sight as they entered the traffickers' territory.

They came upon the first tall plants less than a hundred yards from the river. Most of them were around six feet tall, but several of them had spiraled up above the others, growing toward the sunlight that streamed down through the jungle canopy.

It was a giant Christmas tree patch for dopers. Serrated palmate leaves, small flowers. A garden waiting to be harvested. There were thousands of them, and they were planted in a shifting wall-like pattern that formed a natural barrier.

Tomasa had seen several views of the barrier on the surveillance footage that was shown to them at the Belmopan joint briefing. But it was a different sensation entirely to see it up close. The crop had been planted with almost military-like precision. The aerial recon teams had dubbed it the Marijuana Line, since it reminded them of the Maginot Line of fortifications set up by the French during World War II.

As he looked at the high green plants covering the horizon, a better comparison came to mind. Tomasa remembered his first visit to England when he trained with the SAS at Hereford. On one of his only free days he traveled to see the remnants of Hadrian's Wall, the stone barricade the Roman emperor had built across the narrowest part of Great Britain. It was six feet high and eight feet thick. The Roman barrier had several forts positioned along the way.

He expected to find something similar here. Booby-trapped fields, fortified zones between the fields.

That's why the police commandos didn't rush in. Instead they crept slowly to the edge of the plants, searching the jungle floor for trip wires and the other traps the traffickers planted in their dope forests. Even run-of-the-mill dopers booby-trapped their crops. With hard-core mercenaries, they could expect a lot more.

And they found it.

Coffin hats were suspended high in the trees. The long wooden boxes made of bamboo poles and wooden spikes were held in place by taut ropes that snaked down to trip wires on the ground. The long sharpened stakes were pointing straight down.

A few more steps into the field and some of the men would have been wearing the hats. The heavy wooden crates were designed to drive the spikes down into the head or shoulder of whoever sprung the trap, knock them flat on the ground and plant them into the earth with the rest of the spikes. The result was a blood-splattered coffin. The boxes were long enough and wide enough to take down more than one man at a time.

Aside from reducing their numbers, the grisly mode of death could spread fear through the others.

A couple of men found grenades planted in the crooks of trees. Thin wires ran from the pins and were wrapped around branches. Anyone walking through the branches would have a grenade go off in their face.

Word spread up and down the line about the traps dangling overhead and planted on the ground.

Tomasa gestured for one of his communications specialists to join him, a tall and lithe man with a mop of short dreadlocks. He was known as Azario the Crow and looked like a long-distance runner, but he was their best tree runner. Azario could rapidly scale any of the towering trees that formed the canopy over the jungle. As soon as the man reached his side, Tomasa looked up at the tall trooper and asked, "Any doubt about who we're facing?"

"DOA," the other man said. "Even if they're not, they deserve to be treated the same for what they've done here."

The commander nodded. It had been difficult enough for experienced soldiers to detect the booby traps on the perimeter of the dope field. He tried to picture what could happen to innocent civilians wandering through. He thought of the children back at Tumal's village. The villagers had been warned to stay away from the area, but not all of them would heed the warnings. There might be nothing left of them if they tried to walk through here. And the very same thing could happen to his men right now if they weren't careful.

"Set up the aerials in the trees," Tomasa said to the communications man. "Call Belasko and tell him what we need, what we're going to do and where we're going to be." He passed on a few more instructions, then sent him on his way.

The communications man loped back to the river. Halfway there he slung his knotted rope around a tall thin tree trunk.

Azario tugged on the rope until it was taut, then jumped up and planted his feet on the side of the tree. He started running up the side of it, using his long legs to push himself upward while flipping the rope up like a sling and holding it tight. With a practiced motion he hopped and tugged and climbed up to the top of the tree and poked his head up through the canopy more than seventy feet above the ground.

He unloaded the gear in his pack, extended the aerials, and then clamped them to the thinning top of the tree. One of the major problems in dense jungle was communicating with the other teams in the field. Since the thick canopy often prevented signals from getting through, it was up to men like Azario to incorporate the tree into the system.

He dropped a pair of long wires down to the ground, then went back down the tree faster than he went up, using gravity to pull him downward and the rope to slow his descent.

At the base of the tree he jacked the wires into his communications pack. The looming tree had just become a cell tower and radio station, a giant antenna for the ground team. Azario hooked up with Belasko in less than a minute and passed on the messages from Tomasa.

"Hold on," the American said, conferring with the pilot of the Pave Low helicopter that was ferrying him across the treetops. A moment later he came back on and said, "Can do. We'll be looking for you."

Azario jogged back to his leader's position, slowing and creeping forward in stealth mode as he drew close to the dopers' Marijuana Line.

"It's done," Azario said. "They're ready."

Tomasa took out the compact handheld thermal imager and scanned the dope forest once more. The imager revealed several human shapes on the other side of the barrier. The enemy force had grown considerably in the short time since he'd sent Azario to set up the treetop comm system. Some were directly across from him. Some were spreading out on both flanks.

The doper mercs kept flashing in and out of sight. They were keeping low as they moved through the brush and took up their positions. Getting ready to ambush the Dragon Unit.

Tomasa knew the aerial recon planes and surveillance satellites had picked up a large number of potential enemy targets. Right now most of them were waiting on the other side of the barrier. He knew they were good troops. He believed his men were better. The chance to prove it was imminent.

Tomasa pulled one of the grenades from his web belt, a flash-bang with a lot of candlepower.

All the way down the line his men prepared for the assault, aiming their grenade launchers toward the booby-trapped enemy stalks or arming smoke and stun grenades.

"Now!" Tomasa shouted. He looped the stun grenade high in the air so it came down in the midst of the dope field just as it went off. A loud concussive blast shook the cannabis trees and echoed through the forest. It was immediately followed by several other grenade blasts as his men let loose.

A flash-bang hurricane swept through the field, knocking over the tall stalks and triggering the booby traps all around them.

Four coffin hats plummeted to the ground. The long crates splintered on impact, leaving the spikes sticking harmlessly into the earth. Trip-wired grenades blasted apart the trees where they'd been hidden.

An automatic rifle blasted a swath through the middle of the marijuana patch, but it found no human targets. Anchored to the base of a tree with cordlike vines, the rifle was rigged to empty a full magazine at anyone who tripped the wire tied to its trigger.

After the first round of blasts the Dragon Unit popped several more smoke grenades into the middle of the field. Brightly colored plumes of smoke billowed upward, casting a purple haze toward the sky.

"Pull back," Tomasa shouted.

Expecting the command, the men backtracked through the jungle in an orderly manner.

As they moved away from the smoke-laden dope zone, a few wild shots zipped through the jungle. The doper mercs were firing out of frustration more than anything else. They'd expected the Dragon Unit to waltz into the middle of the field and be cut down like easy prey.

The gunfire stopped when a deafening sound approached from above. Seconds later the Lockheed AC-130 Spectre gunship swooped overhead, guided by the clouds of smoke. As it neared the target zone, the side-firing weapons system poured a blizzard of 20 mm Vulcan cannon fire all the way down the Marijuana Line. At the end of its strafing run it opened up with a 105 mm Bofors cannon.

Any booby traps left on the ground were either tripped or disintegrated.

Right behind the Spectre came two Sikorsky Seaguard helicopters. They dropped tank loads of "red rain," onto the smoky forest. The bright red dyes of the insecticide painted the stalks the color of blood, making them easy to identify from both air and land.

The Pave Low choppers came in next. They followed the muddy waters of the fast-moving river, using it as a road map to bring them into the combat zone. Instead of lingering over the forest and providing targets for any DOA troops in the area, the helicopters swooped down and hovered just above the water near the riverbanks.

Brognola's Special Forces soldiers dropped from the choppers into the shallow water and swarmed up the bank.

As soon as the Americans touched ground, Tomasa led his unit across the bloodred cannabis barrier.

He covered the ground quickly, too quickly perhaps, for he found himself standing in the midst of a surprised group of DOA troopers who'd just risen from their hiding places when he appeared. They were in light green camouflage, and their faces were streaked with mud and war paint. If they hadn't moved, he wouldn't have even known they were there.

Tomasa triggered his short barreled CAR-15 a split second before they reacted. He fired from right to left and two of the men went down, kicked onto their backs by the 5.56 mm autofire. One of the dying men triggered a burst that sliced the air over Tomasa's head and whacked into the tattered dope stalks behind him.

The third DOA gunner swung his rifle toward Tomasa, but the leader was already falling to the ground, instinctively dropping out of the lethal line of fire. The Dragon Unit commander landed hard on his shoulder and for a long panicky second the Colt was pinned beneath him.

Before he could get the Colt free the DOA gunner pivoted toward another target who dashed into the fray. Azario stepped right into a full-auto burst that tracked across his neck like a bloody red clothesline. His head tilted back, practically severed by the heavy metal bullet stream.

Tomasa dived forward and drilled the DOA man point-blank with the rest of his magazine. The DOA man spun and dropped to the ground, as dead as Azario the Crow.

"Bastards," Tomasa swore. "The bloody freaking bastards." He flipped the double magazine and slammed it into place. Then he went deeper into the DOA dope zone, about to bring them the war they were looking for.

12

Mack Bolan crouched beneath the maze of interlocking vines and stepped quietly into the leafy green cocoon.

Long tendrils slapped at his face and slithered across his shoulders as he made his way deeper into the dense jungle labyrinth.

It was like moving through a tunnel of hot humid mist. Sweat soaked through his shirt and pants, making the lightweight fabrics cling to his skin. Clouds of insects drifted in front of him, thickening with every step he took.

Soon a gnat-filled halo was swirling about his face. Some of the voracious bugs parted as he walked by, driven off by the insect repellent that he and the other members of Brognola's team doused themselves with. But an equal number of pests were drawn by the sweet smelling poison, relentlessly stinging him. He ignored the bites of the insects. There were other things on his mind. Estimates placed the opposing force of DOA mercs at anywhere from forty to fifty men.

About forty U.S. Special Forces soldiers jumped from the helicopters with Bolan. Approximately the same number of Dragon Unit troopers were under Tomasa. By rights the attacking force had the odds.

But the DOA knew the territory—the best escape routes, the most natural ambush points.

The dope soldiers had fallen back as soon as the gunship made its pass and the barrage of red rain dropped from above. The maneuvers had successfully cleared the Marijuana Line, but now the ground team was moving farther into unknown territory.

Bolan instinctively avoided the paths the DOA had carved through the jungle on its way to and from the dope fields. There were too many chances to be ambushed along the way or step into some of the traps DOA laid for them. Instead the Executioner and his fellow raiders took the hard way. The slow way. The best way to stay alive.

Even then it was close.

Bolan sensed some movement off to his right and about twenty yards in front of him. It was just a shaking of leaves, a slashing of a branch through the air. But it was enough to trigger his survival instinct.

The quick burst smacked into the tree behind him and chipped off a shard of wood that landed on his face.

He was flat on his back, exactly where his subconscious had thrown him, looking up at the trunk as a second and third burst immediately followed. Two more rows of bullets cored into the hard wood. The bursts kept coming, chipping off more splinters of wood and forming a trail that steadily led downward.

Bolan was already moving. His elbows dug into the marshy ground beneath him and his heels pushed hard into the earth, propelling him out of the killzone and into a small dip in the ground. Still on his back, he slid down on a bed of vines and leaves like a snake shedding his skin on rocks and thorns.

Footsteps sounded on both sides of him as his attackers charged through the brush. The sound was deafening, rhythmic.

The Executioner felt trapped. His heart was pounding and blood was pumping too rapidly in his skull, and he realized he'd been holding his breath. The near-death experience had thrown him off his game. His instinct was to run from the death zone, but that was suicide. If he scrambled to his feet now, he'd be put down forever. All those thoughts flooded his mind in a fraction of second, but in combat a second was an eternity. Long enough for him to calculate his best move.

Instead of running, Bolan stood his ground, lying flat on his back and picturing the attackers dead from his next move. It was part wish fulfillment, part experience. If he didn't believe he had the will to prevail, he was as good as dead. He summoned the brief glimpses of the enemy from his memory and judged the angle of their approach from the thrashing sounds that grew louder and louder.

Only seconds left to live or die.

Bolan clasped the Beretta in a prayerlike grip and fired it upside down in the estimated direction of the DOA ambushers.

The Beretta's 9 mm bursts carved a waist-high arc through the jungle. It was an invisible safety line that gave Bolan room to breathe and time to move. The advancing footsteps had come to a dead stop as soon as he squeezed off the rounds.

He heard shouts from the DOA gunners. A bit of panic and a bit of payback. Now they were the ones on the defensive.

Bolan flipped onto his stomach and kept on rolling, once, twice, moving out of the way.

A shotgun blast raked the brush to his side. Fragments of wood and rock sprayed his face. The exploding earth gouged out droplets of blood from his right cheek to his temple. But his eyes were untouched. They'd caught the flash of the shotgun barrel and his trigger finger squeezed off a head-high burst.

The shotgun dropped and so did the man wielding it. Bolan's bullet trail had parted his hair and his forehead.

Even before the dying man toppled to the ground a burst

of automatic fire streamed over his head and sliced into the brush near Bolan. The DOA shooter knew his pal was dead and no longer had to worry about him. He used the free-falling corpse as a marker to zero in on Bolan.

The Executioner triggered a 3-round burst at the cluster of vines where the barrel-flash had come from. He jogged to his left and fired again at the shape hurtling through the trees.

The man ran to his right, crossing open ground—into the path that Bolan anticipated he would take. The 9 mm slugs took off his bush hat, staining it with blood as it flew in the air.

The dead man dropped into the brush. And suddenly the zone around Bolan was totally quiet.

The Executioner grabbed a fresh magazine from his combat vest and reloaded the Beretta. The click of the clip as it slapped into place seemed almost supernaturally loud, like someone shouting over a loud conversation when the talk suddenly died.

Bolan stopped and listened, knowing that others were doing the same thing. Men on his team. Men on the other side. They were all getting ready for the next firefight to begin.

A multiple volley of bursts shattered the silence. It came from somewhere to Bolan's left. Return fire echoed across the rain forest, ebbing and flowing as the two sides fought back and forth across the dense no-man's-land.

It was eerie during the silences, as if the gods of war were taking a breath before sending their minions into action once more.

Pockets of DOA resistance suddenly rose against the advancing special operations team. They withered under the concentrated fire or pulled back to regroup. Though DOA was suffering a lot of casualties, the hardmen took their toll on the U.S. ops too. Several of them had lain down their lives in the jungle.

Bolan did a slow scan of the area around him. With the heavy jungle growth it was impossible to see more than ten or fifteen yards in any direction. He kept his eyes focused on an area just long enough to decipher any enemy hiding in the brush. It was difficult trying to pick out camouflaged shapes that were the same color as the jungle.

Bolan sensed another man's presence ahead of him, but he couldn't see him. Without moving his head he scanned his eyes left to right, slowly prowling across the jungle for the predator he knew was there.

Dark eyes glistened at him from beneath the broad leafy overhang. They'd seen each other at exactly the same time.

A wild burst of subgun fire spit out from the DOA merc's hiding place, shredding leaves and branches as they burned the air toward Bolan's previous position. The Executioner caught a glimpse of moving brush that made it look as if a tree had come to life before his very eyes.

The gunner had fashioned a ghillie suit, bedecking himself in vines and branches that helped him totally mesh with his surroundings like some dark ancient creature of the forest.

Bolan had dropped to a crouch and fired a burst at the same time as the man in the ghillie suit. The man moved to his right. Bolan threw himself in the same direction and triggered two more bursts. He heard the unmistakable sound of bullets whapping into another man's body.

The man called out just once, his voice choked with blood, then fell to the earth.

The Executioner's immediate threat was gone.

He kept moving in case anyone else was trying to zero into his position. He did his best to filter out friend from foe as the sudden bursts of autofire rattled up and down the skirmish line.

The sounds of war echoed all around him. Men running through the forest, shouting, screaming, dying, clashing in a shifting battle line. Some were retreating, some were advancing, and some of them stayed right where they were, pinned by fire or fear.

Bolan waded into the thick of it.

FELIX TOMASA had tried to keep pace with the rest of his Dragon Unit but the jungle changed his plans. In some areas the secondary jungle growth was so dense it was impenetrable, causing his men to constantly change their direction. It was no longer a solid offensive line. It was a staggered group of elite troopers trying to push the enemy before them. More often than not they couldn't see any other members of their unit.

That's why Tomasa was alone when he saw the shapes fleeing through the dark greenery ahead of him. A cluster of DOA gunners were slipping in and out of the jungle curtain. There was a part of him that wanted to hang back and let some of his people catch up to him. But then he thought of the fallen ones they'd left behind, men who hadn't made it very far past the red rain barrier before a DOA picket line rose as one and hit the commander's people with a withering fire, ripping a lot of holes in their ranks.

There was another force that drove him across the jungle. It was a territorial imperative, a need to eliminate the intruders before they became a threat to his country. But it paled beside the images of his fellow soldiers lying in the jungle never to get up again. Those images were seared forever into his brain. If it had been him lying in eternal silence upon the ground, he'd want someone to seek vengeance for him. He thought of Azario the Crow who'd followed his orders without question. Azario was one of the first to be hit. And he knew that Azario wouldn't creep slowly through the woods while the murderers were getting away.

Tomasa abandoned the caution that had been holding him

back and started running through the jungle, leaping over the fallen trees and ducking under the clinging vines.

It was impossible not to make noise, but Tomasa no longer had to worry about stealth. The group of mercs ahead of him were making such a racket while they thrashed through the forest that their sounds drowned out any of his own.

They were about thirty yards ahead of him when they suddenly vanished as if the earth had swallowed them up. He saw their hands coiling around vines, and then they were gone.

A few moments later Tomasa reached the same spot.

The earth dropped out from under his feet. One moment he was fighting through a wall of dense jungle, the next he was flying in space and grabbing at the vines that snaked down to the ground below.

The sheer cliff had at least a forty-foot drop. Vines dangled in the air from overhead boughs, and a patchwork of ivy covered the crumbling brown rocks of the cliff.

His fingernails ripped through the vines as he descended out of control. He heard a crack as the thumb and index finger of his left hand bent back in an unnatural angle. A burning sensation exploded from inside his hand. Whether something was broken or it was just a bad sprain, the pain was the same. He forced himself to cling to the thick net of greenery with both hands, ignoring the blossoming pain in his left hand.

His uncontrolled fall stopped with a savage jerk as the vines he was riding smashed back against the rock. Tomasa switched his grasp to the cliff-side vines and hung on for his life. The sling of the CAR-15 slid to the crook of his elbow as he swung from side to side. As he spun, he caught sight of the fleeing men.

The mercs were running full speed through a sunken field that had obviously been cleared at one time. It was wide and flat and looked almost like a courtyard except for the irregular clumps of brush that were scattered around. Everything was covered with a layer of dense vegetation. By the way the men moved, as if a single purpose were guiding their every foot step, Tomasa knew it wasn't a panicked retreat. The mercs were heading for a prearranged fallback position.

Tomasa anchored his left arm and elbow onto the ladders of vine and cradled his CAR-15 in his right, trying to bring the weapon to bear on the running gunmen. The vine gave way just as he was about to fire, plummeting him several feet and swinging him back and forth like a pendulum.

Instead of firing wildly and giving away his position, the commander carefully clambered down the vines and jumped when he was about ten feet off the ground.

He came down hard. The impact stunned his knees and the soles of his feet at the same time. His body had been expecting soft earth. Instead it found a massive slab of unyielding rock.

As he jogged across the verdant jungle carpeting, Tomasa realized the terrain remained just as hard as the spot he'd landed upon.

It was a huge foundation of flat blocks covered with moss, scarred with crevices from thick roots that had taken hold in the massive stone mountain.

The ruins.

He'd come to the ancient Mayan ruins they knew were in the area. But the complex was a lot larger than previously indicated on the satellite images he'd studied. He was either crossing a sunken courtyard or the rooftop of a huge fortification.

"Felix! Wait!"

Tomasa turned back toward the wall and saw Titus Pascal, the unit's best crossbow specialist. Pascal waved his weapon overhead and shouted down to him. "We'll help you sweep the area."

Two other BNP ops perched on the edge of the wall and tracked the barrels of their automatic rifles down across the jungle courtyard.

Tomasa waited for them to scale down the wall, knowing that a four-man team had a better chance than a single soldier against the DOA force.

Even before the three men touched the ground another group of Dragon Unit operatives emerged from the forest. They grabbed the vines and rappelled to the level ground.

The eight men quickly covered the ground to the far side of the courtyard. It ended in a wall that was about four feet high. All they could see beyond it was a group of distant treetops.

Tomasa and his men crouched behind the stoneworks and crab-walked along the edges until they found gaps in the wall they could safely look through.

Beyond the wall was a steep hill that led down into the shell of a Mayan stronghold. Crumbled walls, half erect rooms, doorways with stone sills and no roofs. In the center of the complex were the remnants of a large fountain with the curved stone walls mostly intact. Instead of water it was filled with a sea of lush green foliage. Scattered around the site were bunkerlike dwellings and a caved-in temple with a long altar stone.

A ghost town of ancient warriors.

"You see any of them?" Pascal asked.

"No," Tomasa answered.

"Neither do I." Pascal was leaning against the wall and peering out through one of the gaps in the stone. Of them all he had the best eyesight and an almost supernatural ability to pick out a camouflaged enemy from the surrounding jungle. But even he couldn't see any of the mercs on the other side of the wall. "But they're down there. I know it. That's why they were in such a hurry."

Tomasa nodded. The ruins would be hard to overrun. First they would have to make an off-balance charge down the hill, then cross the level ground to the fountain before making it to the other buildings. "Even if we make it, we'll have to fight house to house."

"Ruin to ruin," Pascal said.

The commander looked over at his men. They were ready to go, waiting for him to give the word.

He shifted his Colt to his good hand and took out his pocket scope. He eased back to a V-shaped gap in the wall and peered through. But the field of vision was too limited. The compact thermal imager couldn't pick up any targets. "Can't see from this angle," Tomasa said.

"I just need a general idea where they are," Pascal said as he flattened himself against the wall and scanned the ruins below. "Do a little recon by fire and shake them up a bit. See if they reveal themselves so I know where to go and where not to." He crouched, ready to spring over the side. "Then keep them down while I slip over the wall."

Tomasa nodded. "All right, on three," he said to the rest of the men. "Spray them with full-auto. Save enough for a second volley. And spread out so they think we've got an army here."

His men spread out and took up positions along the wall.

Tomasa shouted out the count. On three they got to their feet, braced their automatic rifles on the wall and hosed the jungle below. They strafed the hillside, the fountain and the ruins with steady bursts.

They dropped back out of sight just as the DOA mercs returned fire. Spears of flame shot up from the greenery. A steady rain of bullets chipped into the wall and burned through the air overhead. The mercs were hidden behind shrubs, behind walls, in doorways, pouring lead uphill toward the Dragon Unit.

Titus Pascal studied the barrel-flashes and fixed their positions in his mind. When the return fire died down, Tomasa shouted, "Again!" The BNP sharpshooters rose once more and laid down a heavy suppressing fire.

PASCAL SLIPPED over the wall and began his quiet descent toward the DOA line while the BNP gunfire kept the mercs pinned down. He stayed low to the ground, inching forward in a slow and steady crawl. The brush was head high in most places, giving him plenty of cover.

He used it to full advantage as he moved inexorably to his first target. Right after the first fusillade Pascal had seen the man pop up from behind a small gully that was capped by a screen of shrub about three feet high. The merc had almost casually strafed Tomasa's position until he'd burned off his magazine. Only then did he drop out of sight.

The gunner's image was fixed in Pascal's mind. He was a mountain of solid muscle with a broad chest, a shaved head and an unshakable belief that he was the meanest son of a bitch in the jungle. There had been something in the man's arrogant stance that drew Pascal's attention, as if he were invulnerable and anyone who dared go up against him was dust. Pascal had seen the type before. Sometimes he saw it reflected in the mirror looking back at him. Most of the time he saw it through a gun or a crossbow sight.

The goliath merc's hiding spot was on the farthest perimeter of the ruins, almost in the forest. Once Pascal got him out of the way he'd be in the safety of the trees, right among the mercs. They wouldn't know what hit them.

But first he had to find out who was invulnerable. Him or the merc.

The crossbow nosed through the brush. It was cocked and loaded with only one bolt, although it could take up to five bolts at a time. He didn't want to waste any of the long bolts, nor did he want to risk making any wild shots that would alert the others.

Right now one was enough.

His left hand cupped the stock of the heavy wooden frame, which was streaked with the green and brown colors of the jungle, the same shade as the war paint on his face that helped him blend in with his surroundings. His right hand pressed on the ground in a push-up motion that quietly levered his torso forward. He repeated the procedure until he was only ten yards from the big merc's position.

His target's head appeared briefly. He was looking toward the wall where Tomasa had lain down the covering fire. The man was so intent on the wall that he didn't expect trouble from any other direction.

Pascal felt invisible, a wraith about to strike down the enemy.

He dug his left elbow into the ground, then gripped the stock until the balance was just right, until the sight of the crossbow was pointing directly at the gully.

Pascal kicked his right foot into the brush.

It made a soft rustling sound. Almost like a footstep. It was just enough to attract the merc's attention. A moment later the shaved head rose above the lip of the gully and looked in Pascal's direction.

He pulled the trigger.

The metal bolt cored through the center of the merc's forehead. A spout of blood sprayed into the air, funneled by the cold steel that performed a surgical trepan on the merc's skull.

The voice came from his right.

"Griffin, what's going on?" It was a heavy British accent. Definitely one of Liege's hard-core mercs.

Pascal dropped his crossbow and scooped up the FAL automatic rifle. A burst of autofire scythed through the trees overhead. He thought he'd bought it for good and was preparing to return fire when the staccato bursts of gunfire moved past him.

Pascal snatched his crossbow and used the commotion to cover his retreat. By now Tomasa and the others were laying down a solid wall of gunfire on the right flank.

Pascal moved back into the jungle about forty yards until he found a good observation post. Then he reloaded the crossbow and watched the forest for any signs of pursuit.

His fate was out of his hands now. All he had to do was wait until the mercs came for him or his fellow raiders caught up to him.

13

The Special Forces unit stormed through the abandoned dopers' camp like space raiders from the next century.

Mack Bolan jogged alongside them as they swept through the hidden jungle encampment, a veteran war horse among the futuristic troopers.

The ops were rigged out with the latest Land Warrior gear provided by DARPA, the Defense Advanced Research Projects Agency.

With their battery packs, M-4 rifles and head-mounted displays, the soldiers looked as if they just beamed down from the mother ship. The monocular displays inside their Kevlar helmets gave them a thermal imaged view of whatever passed in front of the computer-linked vidcam gun sight. The battery packs gave them a charge that was good up to twelve hours.

The Executioner was equipped with the Beretta, a long jungle knife and a belt full of explosives. Enough to get him through the coming skirmish.

He and the troopers quickly searched the encampment, but no matter how sophisticated their viewing capability, there was nothing to be seen.

Judging from the size of the empty camp, there had been about twenty men bivouacked there. It was primitive but comfortable enough for the jungle. The sprawling encampment consisted of simple lean-tos and small huts that were built on stilts that gave them a two-foot clearance off the ground. The makeshift roofs were covered with smoke-browned leaves that served as waterproof shingles.

Some of the dwellings were little more than wooden poles stuck into the ground with tarps stretched taut overhead. Bedrolls were tossed on top of bamboo foundations, which kept them away from the crawling things on the densely matted jungle floor.

Coffeepots and mess kits were abandoned near ash-filled cook fires. Backpacks, bedrolls and cans of ammo were left behind.

Unfortunately, Bolan's frequent radio contact with Felix Tomasa clued him in on the location of the missing mercs.

They were waiting at the ruins.

Bolan and the special ops unit had circled around to come at the ruins from the left flank. That path brought them across a marshy stretch of jungle before they reached the camp.

After scouring the immediate area and the outside perimeter of the camp, they continued on their way, sloshing through the tiny streams that ribboned through the jungle.

The troops conducted a high-tech sweep of the ground in front of them, waving their gun barrels from left to right and feeding the images to the HUD in their helmet. The displays showed the heat signature of every living thing in the forest.

But there were three mercs who didn't show up on the screens—until it was too late.

The trio of DOA gunners rose from the fetid swamp like primordial creatures from the deep, their faces and clothes covered with the muck and vines from the marshy pool. Their rifle barrels slapped down on top of a fallen tree trunk and spit out a furious stream of lead.

The closest trooper caught half of a magazine full in the face. It drilled up through his skull into his helmet and sent it flying in the air. Another volley tracked up his M-4 and smashed the gun barrel video camera to pieces. A final burst hit him as he spun, whacking into the battery pack with a flurry of sparks.

Even before he dropped to the ground the rest of the unit turned on the men who were half submerged behind the log and zeroed in on the muzzle-flashes.

Concentrated firepower poured into the tree trunk and ripped the top half into splinters, and then a moment later it did the same thing to the two men who were still sheltered behind it.

The third man was already running back into the trees. His waterlogged pants legs sloshed through the clinging mucky water, the air filled with bullets. For some reason he thought the ambush would throw the raiders into disarray. After having about three seconds to process the faulty information, he just panicked and ran.

Bullets hit the merc from so many different directions that his body did a crazed two-step, zigzagging back and forth from the multiple gunshots before he plunged into the murky water.

The merc floated facedown among the reeds, a nice catch for any creatures trolling through the swamp.

This was either a planned delaying action or the three men had been separated from the rest of the group when the raid began. After making sure there were no more lethal surprises in the vicinity, Bolan and the ops advanced through the swamp. This time they split into three separate spearhead formations so they could scan the terrain from every possible angle.

There were no more signs of a DOA presence until they approached the woods surrounding the ruins. They picked up images of mercs scattered throughout the forest and the outer buildings of the crumbling Mayan complex. Most of them were partial signatures due to the stone shelters and the rugged terrain.

The thermal imager rigs were good at detecting warm bodies, but they didn't have a hundred percent hit ratio. Bolan found that out when he heard a voice call out his nom de guerre from behind him.

The voice came from an area the troopers had just walked by.

"Striker!" The voice called him again.

The Executioner spun and saw no one until a man with a crossbow rose out of a hole in the ground near the base of a rotting tree. The man pushed aside branches, clusters of mud and broad green leaves he'd covered himself with. "It's me," the man said. "Pascal." As the pile of debris fell away from Pascal, Bolan recognized the man from the Dragon Unit as he stepped out into the open and brushed the last bit of cover from his face.

"Good field craft," Bolan said. "You just got by the best of them."

"I didn't want to startle anyone," Pascal said. "I've been shot at enough today." The Belizean commando told Bolan about his encounter with the DOA when he infiltrated their position. Then he filled him in on the layout of the ruins that he'd seen from the heights of the wall up on the hill.

"How many are left?" Bolan asked.

Pascal shrugged. "They're spread out," he said. "Couldn't get a head count, but there's enough to keep us busy."

The Executioner followed the Special Forces phalanx toward the waiting mercenaries. Pascal cut through the woods on a parallel track.

Less than a minute later the forest lit up all around them as M-4 automatic fire sliced through the woods from every direction. The lead group of troopers had flushed several of the DOA gunners into the open, and now the other special ops troops were picking them off.

The deadly accuracy of the Special Forces' target acquisition system brought down a half dozen mercs in just as many seconds. Simply by looking at the display in their helmets, the troopers could pull the trigger and know they had a confirmed kill. It was a technology that freed them from having to physically look down the sights of their barrels.

The troopers dashed forward, splintering their solid skirmish line as they pursued the targets.

One of the troopers somewhere to Bolan's left shouted in surprise as a stream of fire raked through the trees. The trooper went down as if a buzz saw chopped his legs out from under him. Bolan could hear his involuntary cries of pain as he crawled through the brush.

The Executioner tracked his Beretta toward the enemy's barrel-flashes and caught a brief glimpse of a man running through the forest. The merc fired again from a spot several yards away. Bolan estimated the man's next position and triggered a 3-round burst a few feet ahead of him. He pulled the trigger again to make sure the man ran right into the line of fire.

The 9 mm rounds kicked the merc off his feet and sent him crashing into the bushes.

As Bolan moved toward the fallen trooper he saw several other muzzle-flashes spearing through the far edge of the woods. Instead of retreating, a handful of mercs were advancing on Bolan's position, filling the temporary vacuum left by the troopers. They were moving slowly, but they were definitely moving forward.

Their course would bring them right to the wounded man unless Bolan got him out of there.

The Executioner drifted low through the trees until he saw the Special Forces soldier moving across the ground as if he were doing a broad stroke, clawing his fingers into the dirt and pulling himself a few inches at a time. A pool of blood formed a growing trail as he moved his savaged body

across the ground. His right leg had taken the full brunt of
the submachine-gun volley.

The man looked young, maybe in his midtwenties, but it
wasn't his first time on the battlefield. He was doing his best
to keep his weapon with him as he tried to move away from
the spot where he'd been hit.

The high-tech gear made it difficult for him to make any
substantial progress. Bolan darted forward and gripped the
man under the shoulders, then hauled him back into the
woods.

When he found a small incline shadowed by a layer of
broad green palms he set the man down.

"Go on," the man said, gritting his teeth.

"Nowhere to go, guy," Bolan replied. "They're coming
our way." He looked down at the man's right leg. The autofire had ripped apart his calf and knee. He wasn't going
to do any walking on it for a while, if ever again. But the
Executioner had seen all types of wounds, all types of re-
coveries. "Besides, we've got to stop the bleeding first."
Unless Bolan patched him up soon, the man could go into
shock or die from loss of blood.

"Use my kit," the soldier said, flipping open the canvas
pouch strapped to his web belt. It was equipped with everything for battlefield surgery, including a supply of needles
for the pain.

Bolan took out field dressings, bandages and a pliable
tourniquet strip. He quickly cut away the clothing from just
above the man's knee down to his foot, then applied the
bandages. The bandages slowed the profuse bleeding, but
the blood was still soaking through. Bolan applied the tourniquet a few inches above the wound and tightened it.

Next he removed the man's battery back and propped him
up against a tree trunk to make him as comfortable as
possible.

"Needle?" Bolan asked.

The man shook his head. Sweat was pouring down his face and his lips were shuddering. He was fighting off the nausea and waves of pain that were telling his body to give it up. "Not yet," he said. "I'm afraid if I use anything, I'll pass out. I plan on seeing this through. Just keep it nearby."

"Got it," Bolan said. He put the kit near the soldier, then took another look at the jungle. He couldn't see anything coming, but he could hear them in the distance.

He glanced at the man's rifle and other gear.

"I can't see them coming," Bolan said. "But they're on the way."

"How many?"

"I don't know," Bolan told him. "Could be one or two. Could be enough to overrun us. I'll have a better chance with that M-4."

"It's yours."

The Executioner slipped on the futuristic garb, hooking up the power pack wires to the Kevlar helmet. A while back during some downtime, he'd had a bit of training with prototypes of the supergun and knew the basics.

With the computer hookup, the system could send images to a flying command post that also received images from the rest of the troops in the field. Once the images were uplinked to the surveillance crafts, the airborne crew could assemble all of the combat views and send back a real-time battle map to the ground troops.

Bolan's immediate needs were a hell of a lot simpler. He didn't want to orchestrate a space-age campaign. He just wanted to see the enemy.

He hefted the M-4, swiveling it from left to right to get used to its weight and balance. Even with the video camera mounted on the barrel it didn't weigh much over twenty pounds.

Bolan flipped on the thermal view and swept the rifle back and forth across the forest until his eyesight was acclimated to the video feed that was beamed right to the helmet's monocular display.

The Executioner loaded a fresh magazine into his Beretta and handed it to the wounded soldier. Bolan slapped another full magazine into the man's hand. "Someone will be back for you," he said, then slipped into the woods.

"I'll be here," the man said. "I hope."

Bolan nosed the barrel of the M-4 rifle around a clump of dense brush and moved out. With a practiced movement he swept the rifle barrel in a slow scan, a lethal cameraman scoping out the scene through the electronically linked eyepiece.

Ghosts at three o'clock.

Bolan steadied the gun camera. The thermal imager showed glowing images of two DOA gunmen knifing through the jungle. They were using a row of tall ferns as cover, thinking they were invisible.

The mercs were unseen by the naked eye, but to the M-4 they were lit up targets. Before pulling the trigger and giving away his position, Bolan swept the barrel in a wide arc and picked up two more merc targets. They were coming from the left.

Four of them. One rifle.

Bolan pulled the trigger and hit the two men on his left with a lengthy burst. One tipped over, weighted down by lead. The other man staggered where he stood before crumpling. Bolan kept the M-4 barrel trained on their position just long enough to make sure they were down for good.

The other two mercs had stopped dead in their tracks.

Bolan strafed them with a fusillade that stitched them first across the shoulders. On the backward arc he drilled them in the head. Both of them were dead before they hit the ground.

The Executioner jogged forward over the rough terrain, sweeping the area with the thermal gun sight.

It was clear.

He made it to the edge of the jungle just in time to see several of the similarly rigged troopers moving toward the courtyard ruins, engaging in a running gun battle with the mercs in the courtyard. The gunners fell back into the scattered cluster of buildings.

After a quick scan with the gun camera the Executioner headed straight for the closest ruin. The upper half of the building had been sheared off by time and gravity. The remaining wall was about seven feet high except for an elaborate doorway that was completely intact and supported by thick stone sills.

As he moved along the wall's crumbling exterior, Bolan came face-to-face with a man several hundred years old. He was looking into the grim visage of a Mayan warrior intricately carved into the wall. It was a *stele,* one of several man-high statues that stood in the overgrown courtyard.

The statue jutted a couple of feet from the wall like a guardian at the entrance. Even though it had a foreboding appearance Bolan welcomed the added cover it provided for his approach. The ancient figure had a headdress, scepter and held a long ceremonial sword at his side. A thick-bodied snake was carved on the sword's scabbard, winding around it several times and ending with its fangs open at the blade to add to its bite.

Several other stone faces protruded from the battlement like ancient gargoyles. They'd been carved there centuries ago, but they were still looking out for the enemy.

In this case, Bolan thought, maybe they were looking out for him. The real enemy was already inside.

Staying close to the wall, Bolan eased up to the side of the statue and nosed the M-4 barrel into the open doorway. As he scanned the right side of the ruin the images on his helmet display showed nothing but eroded floors that were overrun with a lot of brush.

Bolan approached the doorway.

Using the technique he remembered from his training, he pressed the barrel flat against the sill and slowly eased his hands forward so he could angle the gun camera across the interior of the ruin. With his hands jutting in front of him as if he were gripping a steering wheel, Bolan scanned the rest of the interior. The technique allowed him to peek around the corner to pick out the enemy without exposing an inch of his body.

Two target images glowed on the monocular display. One DOA gunner was crouched at the corner to his extreme left. He held a submachine gun in his hands, which was pointed at the doorway. He was just waiting for someone to step into the killzone.

The other merc was partially hidden behind some kind of long and wide stone slab. An altar perhaps.

Bolan angled the gun until the sight zeroed in on the man in the corner. Still holding the weapon so he couldn't be seen, the Executioner pulled the trigger. The automatic burst drilled the merc into the crumbling wall.

The man behind the altar fired at the doorway, but his bullets skipped harmlessly across the stone. There was no target he could possibly hit.

Bolan ripped off another burst. The stream of bullets bounced across the altar top, digging gouges into the stone and ricocheting. Stone shards pelted the gunner and sent him sprawling backward. It was enough for Bolan to acquire the target.

He triggered another burst that knocked the remaining merc hard against the inside wall. The impact bounced him off the stone so he staggered forward toward the altar. His hands stretched out as he dived forward onto the slab and skidded across the blood-slicked surface.

Bolan took a quick look inside the ruin, then stepped back out though the doorway.

Waves of gunfire poured down from the high wall above. Bolan turned and saw Tomasa and his men routing a dwindling group of mercs who were trying to escape off to the right.

As the Dragon Unit merged with the special forces ranks the shooting around the ruins gradually died down. The mercs were no match in close-quarter combat.

Within the next ten minutes the combined force of raiders had taken down the enemy or driven off the last one. The crumbling stones had become gravestones for the dope soldiers.

IT TOOK LESS than an hour after the battle for Tomasa's men to clear out several areas where the choppers could land. The wounded and the dead were quickly loaded onto the helicopters and flown back to the hospital station set up in Belmopan.

A second air armada arrived from Ladyville. Several cargo and troop transport choppers brought in a small army of specialists who began the grisly task of gathering the bodies of the mercenaries and searching through their effects. Then they quickly buried them in unmarked graves. No honors or ceremonies were due the terrorists. They'd come into Belize with the intentions of turning it into a cartel haven. Instead they found their rightful places as unnamed ghosts wandering forever around the ruin-filled complex.

While one group dealt with the bodies, a second group swarmed through the dope zone and harvested the cannabis stalks with swift chops of their machetes. The carefully sown fields had brought about death and destruction not because of its inherent dangers but because of the cultivators themselves, who would have poured all of the profits into the coffers of DOA.

Right after one unit mowed down the plants another

group followed behind, roping them into bundles and dragging them in a clearing where huge nets were spread out on the ground. They filled the nets with the massive piles of cannabis stalks, then hooked the nets to helicopter winches.

One by one the helicopters lifted off and carted the contraband back to the downstream village.

The contents of the nets were dumped in a clearing where a controlled burn could be safely carried out.

It was nightfall by the time the Dragon Unit started the burn. The bonfire lapped and roared at the sky like a giant pyre for DOA as the acrid fumes drifted through the forest.

When the fire burned down and the crew doused the ashes, Tomasa and several of his men stayed behind to spend the night in the village. They sat on the expansive front porch of the mayor's house, smoking and talking through most of the night.

Tomasa used the time to try to convince Tumal and his villagers of the need to move out of the area until BNP could guarantee their safety.

For the most part it worked. In the morning many of the villagers climbed into the Panther airboats for the ride downriver.

The mayor stayed on with a handful of villagers who wouldn't be moved from their home no matter what. They believed the worst was over.

Tomasa hoped it was true, but just in case he posted a couple of his men to stay in the village. He knew that DOA didn't take kindly to defeat.

14

Midtown Manhattan

The borrowed limo rolled to a stop in front of the Legacy Building on Madison Avenue. The chairman of Visor Industries was hosting a luncheon and kickoff meeting to plan the execution of their latest South American contract. Airport limos and corporate cars had been dropping off key executives all morning. They'd been flying in from branch offices across the country.

Simon Liege emerged from the limo before the driver opened the door all the way. His longish hair was combed back and tucked beneath the collar of his expensive suit. Armed with a leather briefcase, he pushed through the revolving door.

Liege gave an imperious and dismissive glance to the man behind the security station, which was little more than a glorified information booth. The guard was more interested in looking like a professional than acting like one.

From his experience as a corporate security consultant Liege knew that most major companies had an unofficial hands-off policy. Rather than inconvenience their guests by stopping everyone who came in, security men only zeroed in on those who looked as if they didn't belong.

Liege looked as if he owned the building as he walked to the bank of elevators and thumbed the up button. A few seconds later the door opened with a soft hiss. He stepped into the plush elevator and hit the button for the third floor, headquarters of Visor Industries.

When he stepped out he was confronted with a hivelike maze of office partitions. These were the outer regions of power, filled by lower-rank executives who one day hoped to make it to the inner circle.

By the time he left, they would be glad they hadn't quite made it yet.

As Liege started down a long corridor that led to the heart of Visor Industries, a middle-aged woman in a soft gray business suit looked up from her computer. "Are you here for the luncheon?"

"Yes," he said. "I'm running late."

"You'll have to sign in." She held out a clipboard with a list of names. Liege gently but firmly pushed it back to her. "I'm on a tight timetable. I'll do it on the way out."

She looked uncertain, but the gaze in his eyes had enough certainty for both of them. "Of course," she said. "Go ahead. They're in the conference suite." She pointed toward the hallway he'd been heading for.

"Thanks," he said, and hurried off.

He followed the corridor to the end, where it turned right and led into a small alcove with a thick metal door barring the way. A man stood beside the door. Six foot tall, hair just a bit longer than a military cut, he was the armed corporate muscle with a well-hidden shoulder rig inside his unbuttoned jacket. To most eyes it would have been unnoticeable.

"Coming through," Liege said, manufacturing his best smile and reaching for the door's heavy copper-plated handle.

"You'll have to wait," the man said, pointing toward the electronic pass card system beside the door. "It's controlled access. If you'll just give me your name—"

"Sure. Just hold this for a second." Liege innocently

raised the leather briefcase toward the man, strategically blocking his view.

The guard had just enough time to realize that something was wrong and was about to push the briefcase away when the thin steel blade pierced his rib cage and pushed up to his heart.

"No," the man gasped, stricken by his desire to fight and to keep living.

"Afraid so," Liege said as he stepped forward and covered the man's mouth with his left hand while he pushed harder with his right. The blade made the final cut.

Liege softly let him down to the floor and fished the computer-coded pass card from his pocket. He slid the card through the security slot until a red light came on and the door unlocked. That gave him free admittance for the next thirty seconds or so.

Liege picked up his briefcase. It was time to go to work.

Several heads turned his way when he stepped into the room. The white-haired chairman was standing on a raised platform in the front of the room, gripping the dais as he spoke about Visor's stroke of luck in landing the U.S. government contract. Even though they were just one of several companies supplying the government, the potential profits were enormous.

Behind him a slide show glowed from a large projection screen. It was one of corporate America's beloved multicolored pie charts. It showed the original vendor costs of the armament and night-vision systems that Visor was packaging for the U.S. Department of Defense, as well as the profits, bonuses and penalties. A bar chart below it showed the schedule for final assembly and delivery to the Colombian government.

It was all neatly presented. An extremely thorough plan that appealed to Liege's sense of order.

Unfortunately, the plan hadn't counted on contingencies like Simon Liege.

Liege went to the end of one of the long conference tables that formed a U-shape, with the chairman at the apex. The tables were covered with crystal water pitchers, coffee carafes and the remnants of a catered luncheon. A few of the engineer types and sales execs nodded welcomes at Liege, perhaps slightly envious that he'd been able to miss some of the meeting.

They all wondered who he was, but no one knew he didn't belong.

Liege flipped open the leather briefcase, positioning the raised lid so it screened his hands from the others. He lifted the short-barreled Heckler & Koch MP-5 from its slot, threaded on the sound-suppressor, then slapped in the 30-round magazine.

At the sound of the click two of the men nearest him looked over in alarm.

Liege shot them first.

Then he swept the barrel around the table, mowing down the execs one by one. He continued the sweep, strafing the chairman and sending him tumbling back against the projection screen. Smears of blood spattered all over the pie charts.

Nine dead men later, Liege carefully packed the Heckler & Koch back into the briefcase. He stepped halfway out the door and hauled the well-intentioned but outclassed corporate security man into the room. Then he walked back the way he came.

He stopped at the desk of the woman who'd urgently flagged him down before. She was nowhere to be seen, but her clipboard was in plain sight.

Liege set down his briefcase, and then wrote his initials on the bottom of the list of names.

Right after his initials he wrote down the branch he represented. DOA.

FOUR HOURS LATER Simon Liege was in a top-floor hotel room in Washington, D.C., where he was registered under one of his sanitized identities.

Two of the men who picked him up from his shuttle flight at Ronald Reagan Washington National Airport were staying in the room next to him.

Several other members of the team were scattered around the city making test runs for the following day's activities.

He spent most of his dinner time flipping through the TV channels from one news network to another, sampling the smorgasbord of dismay, outrage and barely concealed excitement served up by the news anchors.

There was no mention of the DOA. The authorities had either managed to cover up its existence or the networks were cooperating. He laughed at the ridiculous thought. Of course the authorities had managed to conceal it.

That left the news anchors playing their favorite game. Was it a disgruntled corporate loner driven berserk after being passed over for a promotion? Was it an extreme case of corporate espionage? A hostile intelligence agency? Though they had little to go on, the talking heads wasted no time in conjuring up worst-case scenarios. Liege laughed when he flipped to another channel and saw a round table of talking heads facing a host who asked them what it could all mean for America.

"It means your time is up," Liege said. He clicked off the remote, sated with the news coverage.

At seven o'clock he rolled the room-service cart outside his door and left the Do Not Disturb sign on the outside doorknob. He strolled down to Union Station, discreetly followed by his two-man security team every step of the way. He wandered around until he found a bank of phone booths.

Inside the last booth he shuffled through the handful of prepaid calling cards in his wallet, inserted one of them and dialed an answering service that had a message from Aaron Priestly. Couched in business language, Priestly was reporting about unexpected losses in the crop futures market and requested a callback at the Gulf office at his convenience.

Which meant it was urgent.

Liege frowned, then used another calling card to make the long-distance connection to Akumal, Mexico, a relatively undeveloped town on the southern end of the resort strip that followed the coast down from Cancun. It was a short jaunt up from the Belize border. It was also Jorge Macedonio's territory. Though other cartels operated in the Gulf region, Macedonio's was one of the strongest.

Liege and Priestly had a few other safehouses in the Quintana Roo province. Beachfront property at Xcacel. A cottage near the ruins at Tulum. The properties were all part of the Gulf office that Priestly referred to. All of them were under the protection of Macedonio.

The fact that Priestly felt the need to go to Akumul meant that something had gone seriously wrong on the home front. His second-in-command wasn't the type of man who was easily spooked. On all the previous operations they'd worked on, he was the last man out. Now it looked as though he was close to bolting.

Priestly picked up the phone on the second ring, as if he were sitting by the phone waiting for someone to throw him a life preserver. "Plant management services," Priestly said. "Marketing department." His voice was slurred. He tried to hide it by talking slow and carefully enunciating his words, but there was no doubt he was on the whiskey train.

"How's business?" Liege asked.

"Down," Priestly said. "Where are you calling from?"

"What difference does it make?"

"Right now it means a lot," Priestly said. "I'd feel a lot better if you were down here."

"I've got a few more stops to make."

"I suggest you make them quick or cut them out all together. We're taking quite a beating in the field." In a roundabout way Priestly told him of the debacle at the camp, speaking about it as if it were a hostile takeover of an agricultural company. Production losses would set them back for years. The cost was in the millions. Their profits were up in smoke and their workforce was permanently downsized. The severance payouts would be extremely high. "I was lucky to escape forced retirement myself."

Liege fell silent as he let the bad news sink in. Severance pay. Death benefits for the mercs who had families. The expense was bad enough, but replacing them would be worse. It was difficult to find the ruthless but competent men he needed for DOA.

He asked a few more questions to make sure he grasped Priestly's meaning. "Do you know who was responsible?"

"Not yet. Could be a leak from our own organization. Could be the locals wanted us out of the area. Whoever it was, they were working with our lifelong competitor."

Liege nodded, thinking of the nearby villagers. He'd been too easy on them. Instead of driving them off they'd tried peaceful coexistence. "Find out who the insiders were and purge them from the organization."

"I'm working on that now," Priestly said. "What about the locals?"

"We've got a reputation to keep," Liege said. "Show them we're the type of company that fights back."

There was silence on the other end of the line. Finally Priestly said, "Are you thinking along the lines of the Karazac business model?"

Karazac. One of the Balkan butchers the Serbian special police units sent in to do the dirty work. Roundups, rapes, massacres, beheadings. Whatever horrors they could dream up. Liege had recruited Karazac and his crew into DOA shortly after they fled their country. The Hague Tribunal had just added them to their growing list of war criminals.

"That's exactly the model I had in mind," Liege said. "Something that makes a statement."

"Done."

"Meanwhile, I'll stay here and make a few statements of my own."

"Make them loud," Priestly replied. "And as I said before, make them quick. Otherwise there might not be anyone left to hear it."

Liege hung up. He understood Priestly's concern. Unless he took care of the home front, the mercenary network he put together could fall apart. But he also understood the need for DOA to strike at U.S. targets. To keep sponsors like Macedonio happy, Liege had to maintain DOA's image as a major threat that could cross borders to deal with cartel enemies.

He'd return home soon enough…after he gave the U.S. something else to think about.

THE FOLLOWING AFTERNOON Simon Liege strolled through the Mall at a leisurely pace just like thousands of other tourists visiting the nation's capital. He stopped by the Reflecting Pool for a while to sit and watch the faces of the people as they headed past him, eagerly chatting about the attractions. The Washington Monument, the National Air and Space Museum, the U.S. Botanic Garden.

All the potent symbols of the country.

All within the reach of DOA.

Liege was most interested in the symbol behind him. The U.S. Capitol Building. In just a short while Senator Hayward was scheduled to make one of his daily "impromptu" appearances on the Capitol steps. He always timed his photo ops so the media would have plenty of time to package the clips for the evening news. As the leading champion of providing U.S. military aid to Colombia and South American cocaine producing countries, he was always in the center of controversy. Always looking for fireworks. After haranguing his colleagues who had the temerity to disagree with him, Hayward would take his customary position on the steps and blast away at his critics.

Liege walked down through the Mall, then headed for Constitution Avenue. He meandered along the avenue and crossed at Sixth Street. Though he looked as if he were just wandering along to seeing the sights, he was actually watching the cars that drove by. Several of them belonged to members of the DOA hit team that was circling the area, ready to plunge the capital into chaos.

It was an elegant plan, he thought, as he rehearsed it in his mind. There wouldn't be a great many casualties if everything went off as planned. He wasn't going for numbers. He was going after a symbol.

One of the leading proponents of using America's armed might to smash the cartels was going to reap what he sowed. He'd often spoken about the threat the cartels posed for the nation.

He was going to find out just how right he was.

Liege looked down at his watch. It was almost time. He began his stroll back to the Capitol Building. By now the news hawks would be gathering. When he reached D Street he climbed into a white van that was waiting for him near the corner.

Sitting in the back seat of the van, he picked up a black leather camera bag that was loaded with 9 mm magazines and an automatic pistol. He slung that over one shoulder, then strapped a broadcast-quality recorder case over the other shoulder, crisscrossing them like bandoliers. The attached microphone was emblazoned with the call letters of a public radio station.

The merc sitting next to him picked up his shoulder-mounted video camera. He looked like many of the other cameramen Liege had seen on battlefields and back streets, a tall scruffy man with jaded eyes. Someone who'd seen it all.

The driver of the van pulled out into traffic and headed toward the Capitol Building. The driver let them off separately, with Liege getting out at a corner and the cameraman getting out at the end of the block.

Liege arrived just as the senator walked to the pocket of reporters waiting halfway down the steps for him. It was a mob of men and women hoping to score a solid news fix.

Hayward brushed a few imaginary specks of lint from his tailored suit. He looked over the crowd of sycophants and nodded to his friends among the press corps, the ones who'd toadied to him the longest. They usually got to ask the first questions, the softballs he could easily field.

Hayward swept a hand through the black toupee that lurked atop his head. Then he preened for the cameras and launched into his latest assault on all the ignorant unpatriotic fools who dared to disagree with his position.

The senator's face blossomed with deep red angst as he mentioned his dear old friend Stephen Allred, the former DEA director who'd been killed at his Maine home by the DOA, a shadowy terror linked to the drug cartels preying upon America.

His eyes glistened with a tear or two just before he segued to the recent deaths in New York City that some of his inside sources believed was also linked to DOA.

As the senator's booming voice peaked the levels of the recorders aimed at him, Liege deftly inched his way up the steps and through the crowd until he came to a stout obnoxious reporter who glared back at him and refused to budge. Liege knuckle punched him in the kidney. It was a short and swift strike that no one else could possibly see.

As the reporter arched his back in pain, Liege glided past him and said, "Maybe you should sit down."

"Maybe you should go to hell," the man hissed through clenched teeth.

Liege smiled at him and continued gently steering people out of his way until he emerged at the front of the pack where a jostling line of reporters shoved lenses and microphones into Hayward's face.

The Q & A session had begun. Liege waited out the first few questions. When Hayward gave the nod to the reporter next to him Liege casually stepped on the man's shoe and ground his heels into his toes. As the man gasped in surprise, Liege pushed his microphone forward.

"Senator, how can you justify sending billions of dollars in aid to the Colombian army?" Liege asked. "This is an army that routinely massacres thousands of their own people."

Senator Hayward sputtered.

Liege plunged ahead. "At the same time you're condemning war criminals in the Balkans, you want to supply war criminals in Colombia with the latest military weapons and surveillance gear."

"This is outrageous!" Hayward shouted. "The government of Colombia is fighting against the cartels. They're attacking Marxist insurgents who want to take over the country."

"Actually, Senator, the army has been sending paramilitary death squads out to rape, torture and kill innocent peasants. After the massacres they plant weapons on the grave sites. It's on the record in case you ever cared to look up the facts instead of using this jingo propaganda to appeal to the lowest common denominator."

Hayward was approaching critical mass. He showed all

the signs of someone whose blood pressure was about to go off the charts. The only thing missing was smoke coming out of his ears.

Usually when he ran into trouble, Hayward just moved on to the next reporter. But this had become a personal battle. To do so now would show cowardice to the public.

Liege stoked him up a few more notches by reminding the senator and the media phalanx about the time a load of cocaine was discovered on the president of Colombia's personal jet. "And what about the two planeloads of cocaine flown into Miami by the Colombian air force? Again, it's on the record if you'd like to look it up."

The reporters turned their cameras on Liege. His attack on Hayward was now the subject of the news conference. They were as shocked as the senator was by the hard-hitting questions. That kind of thing just wasn't done in the capital. Posing difficult questions was asking for exile.

"I will not listen to this communistic disassembling!" Hayward exploded. The idea that someone would call him on the carpet as if he were a mere human being was too much to bear. Usually he could make a reporter back off with a scowl or a raised eyebrow. But this one was too much. Instead of playing the game and fishing for an ultimately meaningless sound bite, the reporter was baiting him.

"We are talking about terrorists. About the kind of people who crept into the home of Stephen Allred who devoted his DEA career to fighting drug dealers at every level. They murdered him when all he wanted to do was enjoy his retirement."

"What about all the people *he* retired?" Liege demanded. "His policies led directly to the murders of innocent peasants by the governments of Colombia and Peru. Just so they could have a body count to show they were winning the war on drugs. Hollow victories like that we don't need."

By now the other reporters sensed that this was going

beyond the debate stage. Hayward realized it as well. There was something about the way the reporter confronted him that made him suddenly feel uneasy. He stared at the strange glint in the reporter's eye, which made it seem as if he were looking past the senator or through him.

"Which brings us to the key question, Senator," the man continued. "If the DOA can take out the former head of your antidrug agency, how can you possibly stop them from striking anywhere in America?"

Glass eye, Hayward thought, remembering the description somewhere of the man behind DOA. The war of words had become a genuine war.

Liege stepped back into the crowd just as his DOA cameraman raised his fake camera over the head of the reporters in the front row and focused on Hayward. The sight was actually a crosshair for the 9 mm automatic pistol built into the camera assembly. He squeezed the pistol grip and caught Hayward in the middle of the forehead with a 9 mm round.

It hit the senator just as he was stepping back, about to turn away. After the recognition he'd wanted to cry for help, but he didn't want to seem weak in front of the media. And deep inside he knew that even if he managed to call for help it wouldn't get there in time.

A piece of the senator's skull flipped in the air as the force of the bullet spun him.

The cameraman fired another shot into the senator's body, just to make sure the man was finished. The last thing DOA wanted was a lingering death where the senator sat in a hospital bed, subject of a media death watch.

Hayward's beefy hands gripped the steps he'd fallen on. But it was just a last gasp reflex. His fingertips loosened, and his bloodied head came to a final rest.

The assassin squeezed off one last shot, purposely hitting the steps so the bullet ricocheted into the crowd.

Cameras dropped and reporters ran. Some of them managed to hold on to their gear and tried to capture the assassin, weighing the odds of catching a film worth a million dollars or catching a bullet in the head just like the senator.

But it didn't matter. There was nothing to be seen but chaos.

The herd mentality had taken over. The reporters ran down the steps, pushing one another out of the way.

Simon Liege was among them.

So was the cameraman.

They ran down to the park and joined the panicked stream of humanity running through the streets. Liege risked a glance behind him and saw a group of armed security men fanning out on the steps and watching the horde stampede in every direction. He laughed. It had worked just as he'd expected. What could the men do but watch and wonder where the shots came from? And how could they single out any suspect when everyone was fleeing for their lives?

Liege kept running until he saw the white van waiting for him in the street. One of the inside men rolled the door open and stood out of the way as he dived inside.

"Where to?" the driver said, looking back at him.

"Home."

Bogotá, Colombia

AT ALMOST THE EXACT same time that Senator Hayward lay dying on the Capitol steps, a car bomb exploded outside an inconspicuous office building on the edge of a commercial district.

It was an adjunct office of the State Security Agency, the very same agency that was due to receive a good portion of the aid promised by Senator Hayward.

The car shattered the front doors and ripped off the walls of the facade. It left a huge gap in the road.

And it left several men from the State Security Agency scattered about the offices in savaged pieces.

Lima, Peru

ONE MINUTE AFTER the Colombian attack, a pickup truck packed with explosives rolled up the front steps of the National Bank of Peru. It was the same bank that hosted an American team of auditors who were helping Peruvian authorities track and seize assets of a Peruvian cartel that provided Colombian processing labs with most of their raw product.

The driver of the pickup truck switched off the ignition, took out the key, and then ran down the street. Two men with automatic weapons covered his escape. A third man casually stood on the sidewalk and pointed the remote detonator at the truck.

The resulting explosion lifted the truck off the ground and left a huge crater below it. It also caved in the walls on the first two floors of the bank. As the smoke cleared, it looked like a three-sided dollhouse. The front was totally sliced off, revealing desks and computers that looked practically unharmed.

Except they were covered with blood.

The trackers had become the hunted.

Within minutes the news went out on the radio and television stations throughout Peru. It was almost the same story that was being covered in Colombia. And both of them were tied in with the attack in Washington, D.C.

Less than a half hour after the Lima attack, a communiqué had been delivered to the embassies of Peru, Colombia and the United States as well as the major new outlets. It demanded an immediate halt to American interventionism in Central and South America. If not, all three countries could expect more of the same.

The communiqués were signed DOA.

15

U.S. Embassy, Belize City

The embassy on Gabourel Lane and Hutson Street was on full alert. Cars on both sides of the street were occupied by plainclothes Agency personnel, ready to intercept any suspicious movement toward the complex.

Reinforced barricades had been set up to prevent any car or truck bomb attacks and the detachment of U.S. Marines guarding the embassy had been doubled.

Special units of the Belize National Police were driving unmarked patrol cars through all of the streets that approached the embassy.

Belize was now on a war footing.

Four of the key men conducting that war sat around a table in a windowless and soundproofed room in the back of the compound.

Mack Bolan, Hal Brognola, Felix Tomasa and Alexander St. Clair were viewing the videotapes of the recent DOA attacks. Though they maintained their silence, each man was in near shock from the audacity of Simon Liege.

The large monitor sat on a wheeled platform at the far end of the table. It beamed down on them like an electronic oracle showing what the future held if Simon Liege wasn't stopped.

Bolan stared at the face of the DOA leader as he stood on the Capitol steps in his guise as a reporter. It was theater.

Guerrilla theater. Not only was Simon Liege bringing them news, he was making the news, putting on a show for the whole world to see.

The leader of DOA knew that ultimately he would be recognized, but as he stood there sparring with the senator he obviously felt totally safe. He also knew that he would appear totally invulnerable after he slipped away from the broad daylight assassination in the heart of D.C.

After the videotape segued to the scenes of destruction in Colombia and Peru, it looped back to the beginning of DOA's declaration of war on the Texas border, showing classified footage of the aftermath of the Del Rio battle. Brognola had assembled a tape of Liege's known attacks. DOA's greatest hits.

Brognola reached for the remote control and turned off the tape.

"Any ideas on how we can stop this lunatic?" the big Fed asked as he looked around the table. "Or how we can find him?"

Tomasa shrugged. The leader of the BNP Dragon Unit knew Liege's habits as well as any man in the country. "He'll find us," Tomasa said. "That's how he works. He's made an enemies list and you can bet that everyone in this room is on it. If Liege isn't in country already, he'll be here soon."

"That's affirmative," Bolan said. "We've got to figure that Liege has absolutely nowhere else to go. It's too hot in the U.S. He knows every agency is out for his blood."

"What about Mexico?" asked Alexander St. Clair, the unofficial adviser to the president of Belize.

"We've been squeezing the Mexican government, holding up aid and military assistance until they give us leads to Macedonio or Liege. So they won't want him around too long."

"There's always England," St. Clair said. "Plenty of people to protect him. He could hide forever."

Brognola shook his head. "It's like Felix says. He has to come back here. If he goes into exile in England or some other friendly place, then everything he's done so far is for naught. No, if DOA is to survive, he'll have to lead it."

The Executioner looked at each man at the table. "The problem is, we can't wait around for him to make the first move. Too many innocent lives lay between him and us."

St. Clair nodded. "Especially after we wrecked his plantation. He lost men. He lost money. And he lost prestige. He'll be looking to get that back in spades."

"Our best chance of stopping him is to be more aggressive in our search efforts," Bolan said. "Overflights, patrols. We need to establish more of a U.S. military presence to find him and flush him out. Unless you think that'll be a problem with your government."

"Oh, it will be a problem," St. Clair said. "But we have no choice." He massaged his wrinkled brow, looking a lot older since the last time Bolan had seen him. Part of that stemmed from the firefight outside the restaurant where he and Bolan had been tracked by the DOA. Getting shot at tended to make middle-aged statesmen think twice about staying active in the covert world.

Another thing wearing down the high-level fixer was the realization that Liege respected no boundaries. St. Clair had spent his whole life building up Belize, and now he was facing someone who would tear it down without a second thought. A dedicated band of terrorists could turn Belize back into a Third World nightmare.

"We appreciate your support on this," Brognola told St. Clair. "We couldn't have hit Liege's field without your go ahead. The same goes for our stepped-up efforts. We can't do what we have to do without your approval. We'll try and keep a low profile, but there are no guarantees."

"Nor is there a guarantee you'll find him no matter how many people you bring in," St. Clair said. "Unless you've developed a few clues I don't know about."

The head Fed smoothed his hands across the table. "As a matter of fact there is. Volos gave us some leads to Liege's Mexican connection. Ever since the Belize City cartel decided to cooperate, we've been zeroing in on Macedonio."

"Volos," St. Clair said, unable to hide the distaste in his voice. "Can you trust him? He's probably just trying to sic you on the competition."

Bolan shook his head. "He's out of business no matter what. He helps us, fine. Then he can walk away from all this as a free man. He crosses us, he goes down like everyone else."

"A wise policy," St. Clair agreed. "But what about the information he provided? Is it valid?"

"Looks good so far," Brognola said. "We've got deep cover DEA agents working with a few *federales* who we trust implicitly. According to their feedback, they're getting close. Hopefully we'll take care of Macedonio soon enough."

"That still leaves Liege on the loose," St. Clair said.

"We're hoping to change that," Brognola said. "So far we've been following up some leads Carvaggio provided us with but we've been doing it very remotely, keeping a discreet watch so we didn't spook anyone."

"And now?" St. Clair prodded.

"Now's the time to throw everything at them. Cut out the places he can run to. Put some fear into his men."

"Can we count on any inside help?" Bolan asked.

"You mean Carvaggio," Brognola said.

"Yeah. We heard anything from him lately? I was hoping he could pinpoint Liege's movements."

Brognola shook his head. "Last contact we had was when

he called with the leads on the eco-tours connection. Those rain forest resorts. He's been incommunicado since then.''

The Executioner knew it didn't look good for Carvaggio, but he didn't want to give up on the man who'd battled beside him. There'd been some pretty tight moments when they fought the Garrison. If it hadn't been for Carvaggio, there was a good chance Bolan might not be alive.

"I know he's been playing a dangerous game with dangerous people," Bolan said. "But there's plenty of reasons for his silence. Could be he's closely watched and can't take any risks.''

"Yeah, Striker," Brognola said. "Could be. But we've also got to consider the alternative. DOA could have discovered he was working with us. That means he's out of the picture permanently.''

"No," Bolan said. "He's still alive.''

"Maybe he is," Brognola said. "Maybe he's still out there in the cold somewhere. So let's put our heads together and see what we can do about bringing him back alive.''

THE GROUND rushed up toward Carvaggio and heat rushed into the cabin.

He was looking out the open window of the tour helicopter as it slowed and flew low above the trees outside of New Albion. The downwash of the rotors etched furrows across the jungle canopy as it approached the barracks the DOA crews were building on the outskirts of the riverfront town. One more imaginary rain forest resort to provide cover for Simon Liege.

The camp looked nearly deserted, which was strange, since the town had seemed too quiet. He hadn't seen any of the mercs trolling from bar to bordello like they usually did from late afternoon on through the evening. The DOA contingent had brought prosperity to New Albion, turning it into a refuge for the hard-drinking whoremongering mercs.

The pilot landed in a clearing in the middle of the compound. The houses that were supposedly being built for the resort hadn't changed much since he'd last seen them. Most of the mercs lived in the primitive housing while the rest of them boarded in the town.

Carvaggio saw two of the men sitting at a picnic table below a shade tree, listlessly playing cards and drinking beer.

"Stay here," Carvaggio shouted to the pilot who'd brought him from Belize City.

"Yes, sir," the pilot said, tossing him a mock salute.

Carvaggio laughed as he jumped out of the chopper. The pilot never got used to taking orders from him. But one of the perks of his ongoing mission was unlimited access to transportation. He frequently used one of the DOA helicopters to ferry him from place to place.

In the past week Carvaggio had flown almost as much as the governor of New York, his old haunting grounds. For a moment he thought of the city, a different kind of jungle that still had a strong hold on him. But Carvaggio was still an exile from there. Too many people were after his head. Seemed like it had been that way forever, he thought. That was pretty common for the mercs in Liege's outfit.

One of the men looked up as he approached the table. A merc whose most recent name was Tom Gray. He was a six-foot-six veteran with a handlebar mustache and a wide brim jungle hat. One side of it was pinned to the bandelero hatband, as if he were a western scout. Instead of a six gun he had a Heckler & Koch automatic pistol in a side holster. He slid a bottle of Beliken beer toward him.

"No, thanks," Carvaggio said, smiling before twisting the top and talking a long gulp. "I'm on duty."

"Aren't we all?" Gray said.

"I guess," Carvaggio replied, looking around at the Spartan camp. "Where is everybody?"

"That's not a good question," Gray said.

The other merc looked up at Carvaggio. Almost seemed guilty. A rarity among DOA. Carvaggio didn't really know these two mercs all that well, but he had more in common with them than the others. They were soldiers, not thugs.

Carvaggio took another long pull of beer to wash away the heat and the dust. "So why's it a bad question?"

"Because you won't like the answer any more than we do," Gray said. "Priestly's been splitting up the crew into smaller detachments, shifting them around the countryside. Only group left in this area was us and Karazac."

"Where are they?"

Gray told him about the orders that came down from Priestly. Ever since the dope plantation got hit he'd been trying to even the score. "He sent Karazac up to the village to smoke the guilty parties."

"Guilty of what?"

"Doesn't matter, does it?" Gray asked. "Karazac will find something even if it's just guilty of breathing the air."

"Why aren't you there?" Carvaggio asked.

Gray looked at him like he was insulted. "I'm a soldier, son," he said. "Not a murderer. Priestly and the rest of them don't seem to make a distinction."

"So you refused them."

"Hell, yes," the big merc said, shaking his head. "I wouldn't follow Karazac to an iceberg in hell."

"What about the consequences for refusing an order?"

"Guess we'll face that if it comes down to it," Gray said. He didn't seem too concerned. "But I don't think Priestly or Liege want to lose any more men than they already have."

"That leaves the villagers on their own."

"More or less," Gray agreed.

"Aren't you going to do anything about it?"

"I already did," Gray said. "I told you about it."

Carvaggio nodded toward the helicopter. "I'm going after them," he said. "Plenty of room for two more."

Gray shrugged. "Refusing an illegal order is one thing," he said. "Drawing on your fellow trooper is another. And that's the only way you can stop Karazac. Open warfare. Of course then you'll have everyone in DOA on your ass."

"If that's the way it has to be," Carvaggio said.

"Do what you want," Gray said. "But me, I'm fond of living. I'm staying."

Carvaggio knew there was no way he could change their minds. As far as the mercs were concerned, they'd done their part by giving him all the information and pointing him in the right direction. What happened from there was up to him.

He jogged back to the helicopter and climbed inside, then thumbed his hand skyward.

"Follow the river," Carvaggio said. "We're going up to the village by the dope farm. You know the place?"

"I've seen it," the pilot said.

"Then take me there."

"In time," the pilot said. "First Priestly wants us to stop off at the tower and check in with him."

"What?"

"Just came in on the radio," the pilot said. "While you were talking to your pals over there."

Carvaggio had an idea it happened the other way around and the pilot had contacted Priestly. But it didn't make any difference. He'd already decided on the course he had to take.

"The village," Carvaggio said. "Now."

"Can't do it. The plan calls for—"

"Your plans just got changed." Carvaggio patted the Heckler & Koch subgun hanging from a chest harness.

"You're a pilot. I'm a shooter. It's better if we don't interfere with each other's job. Just so we don't have any complications." He gave the pilot a look that left him no alternative. If he refused to fly him there, he'd find out just how good a shooter Carvaggio was.

The pilot lifted off, rising over the jungle, heading to the river.

LESS THAN A HALF HOUR later the helicopter was flying low over the brown serpentine river. Its approach was hidden by the primary jungle that flanked the water like tall green canyon walls.

The pilot banked sharply to the left when they reached the backwater that meandered toward the dock near the large main house on stilts.

It looked as empty as the barracks. From the information he got from the pilot and the merc back at the barracks, Carvaggio knew that most of the villagers had been evacuated to Belmopan. But there were still some left.

The pilot slowly circled the village while Carvaggio scanned the ground below with a pair of thermal imager binoculars.

He didn't see a single soul.

And then he saw one that was already departed.

A body was hanging from a tree on the edge of the village near the forest. Head down, hands tied behind its back. It wore blood-spattered camouflage fatigues with streams of blood running down his chest to a dark stain below.

He'd been hanged and used for target practice.

"Looks military," Carvaggio said.

"Belize National Police," said the pilot. "Looks like they left someone to guard the village after they hit the pot field. Didn't do a very good job."

Carvaggio pointed at a patch of level ground near the

scorched remains of the cannabis burn. "Take me down. I'm going to scout around."

"As long as you stick to scouting," the pilot said. "You interfere with Karazac's job and—"

"And maybe we can hold our heads up when this thing's over," Carvaggio said.

The pilot wasn't interested. He'd been on too many scorched-earth operations to care about a few more bodies.

He took the chopper down, and then he nodded with his usual detached manner when Carvaggio told him to wait for his return.

But as soon as the former hit man reached the steps of the first building, the pilot lifted off and headed for the river.

Carvaggio swore as he heard the fading echo of the rotor blades soaring across the jungle. But he'd expected it. The pilot was ultimately Priestly's man, not his.

The inside of the main house was empty, but there was food on the table. Three places were set. The plates were half full. Whoever had been here left in a hurry.

Carvaggio quickly scanned the rest of the houses, found them empty, then walked to the woods. He stopped before the thick tree limb where the dead soldier dangled from a thick green vine that had cut into his neck.

There were bullet holes all over his body, tracing a path up one leg and down the next. The wounds were carefully placed as if he'd been killed a piece at a time. There was nothing he could do about him now.

It wasn't a glorious end but it wasn't totally unexpected. Soldiers knew the risks they took. Still, Carvaggio thought, it was undeserved. If anyone deserved to be removed from the earth, it was Karazac.

He looked up again at the body. An unmoving feast for insects. A glimpse into his own future, perhaps. The smartest thing to do right now would be to forget about it. Drop the hunt. This wasn't his fight. These weren't his people. But even as the thoughts came he knew it was just his instinct for self-preservation kicking in. He didn't have to confront Karazac. He could simply wait around and do nothing, then go back to the DOA barracks. Or he could make his way to Belasko or Brognola somehow.

Get out of the jungle.

Get out of the madness.

But there was something else driving him. It was the same thing that made him an outcast when he was with the Garrison. He wouldn't take an innocent life back then and had to fight a war with his own people because of it. In his mind, soldiers in Mob crews were fair game. Everyone else was off limits. Carvaggio was the only one who saw it that way, but he knew he was right and they were wrong.

The same rules applied to Karazac and his men. Especially them. They were former members of UDBA, the notorious Serbian Internal State Security that sowed terror throughout Bosnia and Kosovo. Beheadings, bludgeonings, rape, torture and murder were just some of the specialties of these ''special police'' who were dispatched directly from Belgrade. Nothing was out of bounds to them. Any survivors from the village would quickly find that out.

Carvaggio took one last look at the hanging man, then walked into the jungle. There was no other path he could follow and still live with himself.

He quickly picked up a trail that was made by people moving in a hurry through the dense foliage, the kind of trail made by people running for their lives and the hunters chasing after them. Broken branches, trampled brush, heavy footsteps in the wet humid jungle floor.

A quarter mile from the edge of the jungle Carvaggio came upon the first casualty.

It was an old man lying flat on his back.

The man was bald except for patches of white hair. White hair speckled with red. It looked like the side of his head had been caved in by a rifle butt. He was looking up at the sky with his eyes wide open and unafraid.

At least the villager had been killed quickly, Carvaggio thought. And it obviously happened in combat. For beside him was a body of one of the mercs Carvaggio had seen in the barracks. There was a long knife wound in the man's chest and a bloody gash in his throat.

The old man looked strong and agile for someone of his age. He probably had surprised his captors who figured he was easy prey.

Carvaggio continued moving deeper into the woods, scanning ahead of him with the thermal binoculars.

And then through the bright green thermal imager screen he saw a few forms moving in the jungle ahead of him. Three men, maybe more. Another figure was struggling with them.

At the same time he heard a woman's scream.

Loud whirring drumbeats drowned out the scream moments later as a helicopter approached from the river.

No, Carvaggio thought. It wasn't coming from the river. It was coming from the other side of the jungle. Soon the thrumming rotors echoed from all around him. He looked up and saw the tour chopper streaking across the sky almost directly overhead.

And then he saw two other helicopters circling over the trees. They'd come to stop him or bring him back into the fold.

It was too late for that.

Carvaggio jogged through the woods toward the figures he'd seen through the thermal imager. He didn't worry about the noise he made as he pushed through the clinging vines and slashing branches. The sound of the choppers and the woman's pitiful cries covered his approach.

He stopped at the edge of a small clearing where Karazac

stood over a young mestizo woman. She was half naked, beaten, struggling to get to her knees.

There were two other men with the Balkan merc. They stood on each side of her, taunting her with loud coarse voices, reaching out and pulling her long braided black hair as if it were a rope. She couldn't understand a word they were saying in their native tongue, but she pleaded with them anyway.

They laughed louder, savoring the terror in her eyes and the quaking in her voice. Suddenly Karazac reached down and grabbed her beneath the armpits. He yanked her aloft and held her over his head like a trophy.

In a parody of a dance he spun her so that her body continually bashed into the other two mercs. They slashed at her clothes, tearing off a bit more with their hands each time she swung by them. Then they held the tattered rags in their hands like captured flags.

It was a ritual they'd developed over their years.

A ritual that earned them this long overdue rendezvous with Nicholas Carvaggio.

He shouted Karazac's name, knowing what was bound to happen. Karazac and his men weren't the kind of men who would stop. They would challenge whoever dared to interrupt their sport, and that was exactly what he wanted.

The Balkan butcher turned suddenly, his face twisting into an ugly scowl as he saw Carvaggio aiming the barrel of his Heckler & Koch in his direction.

"Let her go!" Carvaggio shouted.

Karazac laughed. "Whatever you say!" he bellowed. He tossed her in the air like a rag doll. At the same time he reached for his weapon. The two mercs beside him were already going for their subguns when Carvaggio opened up.

The 9 mm rounds from the Heckler & Koch thwacked chest high into the first merc and kicked him flat on his back. The merc's weapon fired straight up in the air, then came to a sudden stop.

Carvaggio kept sweeping the barrel in a horizontal motion as he triggered the subgun. A volley of bullets stitched Karazac across his massive gut and made him spin in his final dance upon the earth.

In a continual motion Carvaggio bore down on the last merc and caught him with a shoulder high burst.

The wounded gunner stood his ground and returned fire with a full-auto burst that raked the trees around Carvaggio. Then the man ran several yards and dropped out of sight.

Carvaggio circled toward him. Halfway there a huge shadow fell across the field. A helicopter was looming above him, stirring the treetops with the downwash.

He caught a glimpse of Aaron Priestly in the front and a few more shapes in the back bench. A moment later Priestly's voice boomed from the helicopter's amplified speaker. "Put your weapons down! Everyone put your weapons down."

Carvaggio saw the woman running across the field.

Good, he thought. She was out of the line of fire. Out of the hell the Balkan mercs had cast her into.

He aimed his submachine gun at the high grass where the last merc had fallen and triggered two more bursts. There was a sudden burst of return fire and then dead silence.

Carvaggio burned off the rest of the clip, changed magazines and then stalked toward the killing ground.

On his way to the wounded man he came upon the leader of the Balkan mercs. He was still alive but unable to move. His breath was coming in ragged gasps and his eyes burned into Carvaggio with demonic intensity. He'd never believed that death would come to him.

Carvaggio made a believer out of him with a burst that caved in his skull and drilled his gray matter into the ground. It was overkill, but it was unavoidable. Appropriate last rites for a man like Karazac.

The helicopters were circling over the jungle like birds of prey. He saw a barrel protruding from the cabin of Priestly's cabin as one of the gunners took aim at him.

Carvaggio saw high grass moving off to his left. He charged at the remaining man's position and raked it with several quick bursts. A spear of flame shot up from the grass and a stream of bullets singed the air near Carvaggio's head.

Then the rest of the man's clip burned off, thudding into the ground. By the time Carvaggio reached him, he was dead with a fresh trio of bloody red bullet holes on his chest. His hand held the submachine gun in a death grip.

He looked the best Carvaggio had ever seen him.

Their reign of terror was over.

Carvaggio ran back into the woods just as Priestly's helicopter angled for a descent near the slain mercs.

Let him try, Carvaggio thought. The terrain was too rough, and the clearing wasn't nearly wide enough for the wide diameter of the rotors. Just a few rotor blade whacks into the treetops could send the chopper crashing to earth.

The pilot had to have realized it at the same time. He ascended at an angle that brought him back over the jungle.

Through the distant curtain of forest Carvaggio saw one of the other helicopters landing in the village. There was plenty of space there. The other gunships would probably follow suit, he thought. Or maybe one would track him from overhead while the ground troops herded him through the brush.

Instead of panicking, Carvaggio set out on his course. He'd been in this same predicament many times before.

Running through the jungle.

SOMEONE WAS in front of him.

Carvaggio caught the flash of movement through the binoculars. It was off to his right. A man was dropping in and out of sight as he moved in a horizontal line that would cross Carvaggio's path.

The merc was carrying an automatic shotgun with a revolving drum barrel. With that kind of firepower he wouldn't have to be too close to take down Carvaggio.

The former hit man waited for him to pass, carefully watching the man's ghostly transit as his thermal image appeared and disappeared from view. Just as Carvaggio was about to move again the man came back. He was ducking and reflexively seeking shelter.

The DOA gunner was patrolling a grid and ready to take down Carvaggio when the others flushed him out. And that wouldn't be too long. The helicopters had dropped off at least six or seven men in the village, maybe more, who were now somewhere behind him, beating the bushes for him.

And they'd obviously dropped off others ahead of him.

If Carvaggio waited, the men behind him would surely find him. If he shot the man ahead of him, the others would know his position.

Ultimately, he wanted to get to the river and work his way back down to New Albion. But he knew they'd be looking for him by the water. His only hope was to keep going straight into the jungle.

Straight past the sentry.

"Okay," Carvaggio said under his breath to the merc. "You win. You get first crack." He waited until the man was almost on his extreme right and looking the other way. Then he loped forward, gauging the speed he'd have to maintain to make it past the guard before he turned.

Just enough time to make it, he thought. Freedom was another twenty yards away.

But the man turned suddenly, alerted by some sixth sense or maybe by the sound of Carvaggio's flight. It didn't matter. He'd been spotted.

The man swung the barrel of the automatic shotgun toward him, firing a few degrees too early. Shotgun loads ripped through the trees and brush off to Carvaggio's right.

Even as the rotating drum barrel blasted several more high-explosive rounds at him, Carvaggio zipped the mercenary with a burst from the Heckler & Koch. The well-aimed volley caught him head-on. His back arched in a violent angle, and he stood there as if he'd been electrocuted. The shotgun wavered, but he was still trying to bear down on Carvaggio.

He triggered three more rounds into the gunner, who staggered sideways and dropped into the brush.

The exchange of gunfire was like a magnet.

A lead magnet.

Spears of flame pierced the green wall of jungle that curved behind him. Everywhere he looked he saw a barrel-flash illuminating the shadowy jungle. Bullets whined overhead, cutting down branches, thwacking into trees, burning the air by his head much too close for comfort.

Gunfire was one thing. He'd been in combat before and knew that the key was not to panic. But all of that logic vanished when the treetops started crashing down in front of him, slashing through the upper branches like a guillotine.

Carvaggio was running on automatic pilot before he realized what was happening, jumping over the massive trees that fell in his path and dodging the thick limbs that hissed down from above.

Then he looked up and saw the scout helicopter hovering above him.

A chain gun was firing through the high canopy as it cut down his avenue of escape. His quick glimpse showed that the chain gun was the least of his worries. The helicopter's weapon platform also had a rocket pod that could vaporize the ground around him.

Carvaggio snap fired a few bursts at the cabin, but it was

instinct that made him do it, not common sense. He didn't have the time to aim properly with so many bullets burning the air around him.

The chain gun chopped a brace of trees in front of him, herding him off to the left.

Shouts echoed behind him. They were closing in.

Any second now he'd catch a bullet in the back. It was inevitable. But the thought of being shot down like panic-stricken prey was too much for him to bear.

Carvaggio slowed his pace and searched out a tree thick enough to provide cover. Still gasping for breath from the hunt, he leaned against the tree and leveled his H&K in the direction he'd just come from.

They were coming on fast. He could hear their footsteps, sense the blood lust. He was ready to step out and take down as many as he could before they cut him down.

Now that he'd made his choice all of the fear melted away, banished from his soldier's bearing. He'd always done things right. And this was the right way to go. Carvaggio exhaled and was about to step out into the open when he heard a footstep behind him.

It was just a footfall on the wet jungle floor, but it was enough to alert him. He spun just in time to see a flash of smooth and dark polished wood swinging toward his face.

Carvaggio dodged to his right.

The rifle butt followed him. It caught him square on the side of the head, smashing into his cheek and temple and causing his eye to explode in terrible wet pain.

The blow lifted him off the ground.

As he fell, he saw his attacker following through with the swing. He'd hit him broadside with the rifle as if it were a baseball bat.

Carvaggio tried to raise his arm in defense, but his body was no longer following instructions. His hand flopped weakly at his side and he landed on his back.

He looked up into the weathered emotionless face of a hard-line mercenary about to finish what he'd started. Just a craftsman doing his work. The merc raised the rifle over his head like an ax and chopped the hard wooden stock down on his leg.

Carvaggio was already fading from the hit to the head, but just before he went out he heard the crack in his leg. Molten fire spread throughout his body and seared toward his brain.

And then he felt himself being pulled under as he floated away on a river of pain.

16

Quintana Roo, Mexico

"We've been made," Hernandez said, pressing down on the gas pedal as soon as he saw the bright headlights shining in his rearview mirror. He whipped the late model SUV around a sharp bend in the winding coastal road.

"Maybe," the man in the passenger seat said. "And maybe it's our opposite numbers." He looked back through the tinted rear window at the distant lights. There was no reason they should be singled out for pursuit. Their SUV looked just like many other vehicles on the beach strip. The kind of car driven by people who made it rich in the drug trade.

"Doubt it," Hernandez said. "Too much time passed since they missed the rendezvous. They're gone."

Gone.

Neither of the DEA officers liked to think about what might have happened to their *federale* contacts. In Mexico there was always a chance the antidrug police would be picked up by the real drug police, the corrupt ones who worked for the cartels.

Hernandez lightly gripped the wheel as he rocketed past the villas and hidden fortresses that had been built along the meandering coastline of the Yucatán peninsula. To the left was the ocean, sparkling waves gleaming in the moonlight. To the right were dark patches of forest and thousand-year-old ruins. Graveyards, he thought. Maybe with a few vacancies just waiting to be filled.

This stretch of road was strictly upscale. Very private. Very dangerous. It was rife with police protection, the kind that protected drug shipments, the kind that abducted potential enemies of Jorge Macedonio. Until this night the California-based DEA officers believed they were safe. Both of the deep-cover operatives were of Mexican descent. They spoke the language perfectly and could pass for locals in most places.

But this coastal zone wasn't most places. Proof of that were the headlights that reappeared behind them shortly after Hernandez roared down a long straightaway.

The vehicle was a lot closer than before, and it was gaining speed.

"They're going to try to take us," Hernandez said. "Let the man know."

The passenger flicked a button on the dashboard. A tray slid out with a digital keypad and slim handset. The DEA undercover vehicle had GPS, satellite links and radios. Everything they needed to make direct contact with Brognola's team, which was en route. He tapped a preset button and made the scrambled secure connection.

"Striker, this is Beachcomber," he said. "We lost our welcome wagon and are being pursued by unknown subjects. Heading south two miles below Macedonio's villa. Lot of activity going on there. So far three choppers have come in and two have gone out. There was a convoy of vehicles outside the villa. That's where we picked up our tail. We are going to evade if possible. If not, it's going to get real loud down here."

Striker's voice came in loud and clear. "Understood, Beachcomber. We're on our way in. We'll be looking out for you."

A NIGHT STALKER detachment from the U.S. Army 160th Special Operations aviation regiment flew fast and low over the sea, keeping a low signature as they bore down on the Yucatán peninsula.

The black helicopters carried black-clad special ops soldiers who were used to carrying out midnight runs like this. Their mission was to come in fast and silent before anyone knew what hit them.

Bolan was riding in the lead chopper, sitting on the back bench and viewing the cockpit displays of the target zone. He was the link between Brognola, the SOAR unit and the DEA team on the ground.

Satellites and high-altitude reconnaissance planes had been feeding steady streams of intel to the helicopters from the moment they left Ladyville Airport back in Belize. The entire Yucatán region had been under intense surveillance ever since the DEA ground team learned from their Mexican contacts that Aaron Priestly had been seen in the area shortly before a tour chopper spirited him away.

The tour company supposedly flew high paying tourists from Cancun and Cozumel back and forth to the ruins that dotted the landscape throughout the Yucatán. But in reality it was a front company for Jorge Macedonio, a private air force that served the Quintana Roo cartel. It was the primary method for ferrying Macedonio across the border with Belize and Guatemala. Brognola's intelligence showed that the same front company just happened to own the tour helicopters that DOA used to cover their activities in Belize.

It looked as if the heavy surveillance was finally paying off. There was a good chance that Macedonio was in residence at his seaside villa. Possibly Simon Liege was there. Or maybe they were both already in the air. It didn't matter. The other helicopters would be tracked every inch of the way.

Unfortunately, the people who helped them zero in on the

villa were unaccounted for. The *home team,* the DEA's code for the *federales*, had been taken out somehow. Bolan felt for the Mexican nationals who'd given their lives in the attempt to shut down the Quintana Roo cartel. They had the worst fight of all. Not only did they have to combat the drug traffickers, they had to combat their own police agencies. He couldn't bring them back, but he could make sure their killers paid for it.

Bolan picked up the sat-com unit and bounced his call back to Brognola who was coordinating the two-pronged operation from Belize. One helicopter squadron was coming in from the sea to launch the strike. The other squadron was lurking just across the border, keeping tabs on the other tour choppers that had already left Macedonio's villa.

"It's about to go down," he told the head Fed. "Any moment now and we'll be at the point of no return."

"It's still a go, Striker," Brognola said. "Stay the course."

"That's a roger," the Executioner said.

As he cradled the handset, he looked out at the dark water blurring below him. He and the special ops team were about to breach sovereign territory. Bolan and Brognola had discussed it for hours with their Belizean counterparts. But in the end they knew they had no choice. Maybe some people would call it a crime. But if the government of Mexico was harboring a narcoterrorist of Macedonio's stature, who in turn provided support for DOA, it would be a crime if they didn't go in.

There was always a chance of political fallout. But along with state-of-the-art weaponry, the Night Stalkers were equipped with advanced video cameras that would document for the whole world what was going on in the Yucatán compound. The world would have to wonder how a terrorist and drug trafficker with so many Mexican police working for him could be virtually invisible to the government. No,

Bolan thought. They wouldn't be so eager to make an international incident of it.

If they ever found out what hit them.

Bolan punched up the display screen and zoomed in on the images of the DEA vehicle and the pursuit car.

And then he saw a third vehicle suddenly swing out onto the road about a mile ahead of the DEA's vehicle. It came to a dead stop just around the turn at the end of the straightaway, then parked broadside across the road. A handful of figures scrambled out of the car and took up positions on both sides of the road.

Bolan zoomed in the display and saw the ambushers leveling their weapons at the curve in the road. Any doubts that the DEA officers were targets were gone.

"BEACHCOMBER, this is Striker. You've got company dead ahead. They're blocking the road around the next turn."

Hernandez swore and let up on the gas.

"Deal with the pursuit car," Bolan continued. "We'll take the others."

Hernandez looked at the man riding shotgun. "You ready for this?"

"Since we got here." He reached down to the customized well that was built into the side door below the armrest and lifted the FA MAS Commando rifle. The short-barreled 5.56 mm Fusil Automatique assault rifle held twenty-five rounds and fired at a rate of 1000 rpm. To help control the compact automatic weapon he flicked the selector to burst mode.

His right hand curled around the finger grooves on the pistol grip as he rested the chopped barrel on the open window.

Hernandez looked in the mirror, saw the chase car rapidly gaining on them. He hit the brakes and spun the wheel in a controlled skid that turned the car around in a 180-degree arc.

As the SUV's smoking tires screeched on the asphalt, the pursuit car tried to stop, but lost control. It skidded past the SUV, swerving across the lane. It was a police car with two uniformed officers bent on murder. One of them stuck a pistol out the window.

The FA assault rifle opened up, severing the crooked cop's hand with a rapid succession of quick bursts.

The DEA shooter followed the skidding car with a withering volley of 5.56 mm slugs that put down the closest cartel cop for good. Without letting up, he triggered two more bursts at the driver who was now wrestling with the out-of-control steering wheel. The bullets scythed across the front seat and drilled the driver in the skull.

The police car went off the road, rolling over several times before bouncing to a final stop, upside down with a pair of dead cops embedded in the crushed rooftop.

Farther down the road the ambush team double-timed it around the bend just in time to witness the carnage.

They were just about to head back to their car when the black helicopter swooped down out of the night and hovered above them like a giant bird of prey.

For a fraction of a second they glimpsed the faces of death that came down to them in the darkness. Black-clad commandos, every one of them an expert marksman, aimed automatic weapons at them.

The stunned would-be ambushers raised their weapons skyward. They were acting on reflex, realizing that they were the ones who fell into a trap, and there was no way they could get the drop on the professional soldiers above them.

Dozens of barrel-flashes lit up the inside of the helicopter as the commandos poured a blizzard of lead down upon Macedonio's men.

As if a huge wave washed over them, they all fell at the same time, drilled into the road by the automatic fire.

The Night Stalker flew straight down the road and landed just past the SUV. Both of the DEA officers raced for the cabin, jumping in to the outstretched arms that hauled them aboard. Moments later they were airborne, trailing behind the rest of the helicopters that were soaring toward Macedonio's villa.

THE AH-64 Apache gunship streaked toward the walled-in courtyard. At the last possible moment it pulled up and hopped over the wall.

It was a simple feint designed to determine if the group inside the villa was hostile and what kind of firepower they had.

The answers came in the brief instant the chopper was over the courtyard. Small-arms fire chased after the Apache as Macedonio's men emptied their pistols skyward. A burst of subgun fire rattled harmlessly off the side of the armor plated gunship.

Then came the rest of the squadron.

A Bell AH-1 Cobra ripped 20 mm cannon fire through the tour helicopter that sat in the middle of the wide courtyard. Seconds later a rocket slammed into the grounded gunship and blew off the rotor. Whoever planned on flying out of there had a sudden change of plans.

Two more Cobras soared past the villa, hitting them from both flanks. Heavy-caliber machine guns turned the courtyard into a fire zone. After the pair of Cobras made their pass the Apache looped back and unleashed a pod full of high-explosive rockets into the villa.

The walls and gates crumbled. Clouds of smoke plumed above the villa. Like insects flushed out by an exterminator, the cartel gunmen ran out through the trashed gate. Once they reached the relative calm outside the smoldering villa walls they regained some of their poise. A handful of the men formed a protective phalanx around a tall and unmistakable figure.

Jorge Macedonio.

Mack Bolan stepped from the shadows as soon as he saw the leader of the Quintana Roo cartel, the man who had helped orchestrate so much slaughter.

At the last instant Macedonio felt the eyes of the Executioner upon him. The broad-shouldered man picked Bolan out from the DEA officers and the black-clad commandos by his side.

He felt his impending death. Torn between warning his bodyguards or aiming a weapon at the Executioner, he ripped an automatic pistol from a side holster and brought it to bear on Bolan.

The Executioner trepanned his skull with a well-aimed burst from the Beretta. The three 9 mm rounds knocked the big man several steps back. His hands swept wide, clutching for the support of the cartel enforcers. They turned and stared, shocked at the sight of the man whose force of will and force of arms had brought them this far. They backed away and let the bloodied corpse of Jorge Macedonio dropped to the earth.

His men followed him moments later, ripped apart by the precisely aimed weapons of the special ops team.

It was suddenly silent. Nobody moved. Nobody returned fire.

They hurried forward and searched through the bodies, looking for a blond-haired man with the glass eye.

Liege wasn't there.

Bolan headed back to the helicopter that had dropped him on the road outside the villa, then called Brognola at his command station in Belize.

"He's not here, Hal," Bolan said after reporting on Macedonio's death. "Liege is nowhere to be found."

"That means he's probably on his way home," Brognola

said. "We've got the two tour helicopters under surveillance. Both crossing the border into Belize. One's heading for an old radar complex that's been turned into a rain forest lodge. Looks like the other one is heading straight for New Albion.

"So are we," the Executioner said.

New Albion, Belize

NICHOLAS CARVAGGIO woke in a cloud of stillness. Voices were floating somewhere nearby. Two men. One of them was Aaron Priestly, the man who'd led the hunt against him in the jungle.

The image of the big merc swinging the rifle like an ax suddenly came back to him. And with the image came the tremendous pain.

The side of his head throbbed. His leg felt splintered. His knee swollen and useless. There was a constant aching, burning sensation up and down the left side of his body, as if his nerves were pulsing with overload.

His eye felt swollen and caked with blood. He hadn't opened his eyes yet. Instinct had kept them closed. As his senses came back, he tried to figure out his location.

He was in a bed somewhere beneath an overhead fan that stirred the hot air in the room. Half dead. Maybe more than dead. Priestly and another man were at the far end of the room. Conducting a death watch, he thought. But for some reason he'd come back from that dead zone.

No matter how much he wanted to drift back into painless unconsciousness he had to hold on. The two men were discussing him.

"I say if he hasn't come around yet, he won't be coming around at all."

"Because of you," Priestly said. "You hit him into next week. Christ, you hit him into the next world."

The other man swore. "If a man's got a gun, you don't give him a love tap. What's done is done. I've seen enough like him before. Coma, internal injuries. If he does wake up, he could be a basket case. Let's just do him and get on with things."

"No," Priestly said. "Not until we find out what he knows. It could be valuable information. Especially if he's been working both sides of the trail."

"He's your prime candidate?"

"Someone's giving out information. We get hit every time we turn around."

"Yeah, well, I blame that on Simon. If he stayed here where he belonged—"

"He's on his way now. Let him decide when he gets here."

Carvaggio heard the clinking of a bottle and a couple of glasses. There was a pause in their conversation just long enough to drink a couple of shots.

"What are you thinking, Aaron?"

"What if he's faking?"

"I'll check him out, then."

Priestly laughed. "Not on your life. You'll kill him with your soft touch. Let me."

Carvaggio mentally steeled himself for what was coming, but at the same time he forced his breathing to remain even.

He told himself to keep his eyes shut as he heard Priestly's heavy footsteps approach, felt him leaning over the bed. A heavy hand dropped to his knee and pushed down. The knee felt numb though. He felt he could handle it.

But the attack came elsewhere.

Half of Carvaggio's face was ripped off. It was accompanied by a loud tearing sound that lifted his head from the bed.

Blood poured down the side of his face and flooded his

left eye socket. Through a liquid red haze he caught a glimpse of Priestly holding a bloody scalp in his hand. Or so it looked. But as he fell back onto the pillow he realized it was a bandage that the DOA lieutenant had torn from the side of his head. He sank numbly back down on the bed.

"Still dead to the world." Priestly said. "But he'll come around. Simon will see to that. Come on. Let's go see to the troops."

"What about his face? He's bleeding all over the place."

"Send Florence Nightingale back in."

As soon as the door opened, he heard the sound of bar life. Men shouting too loud. Women falsely protesting. Loud jukebox music drifting into the room.

It could only be one place, Carvaggio thought. The St. George Bar and Hotel in New Albion. When the door closed he opened his eyes and looked around the room. It was familiar. One of the upper bedrooms the girls used for entertaining purposes.

His hospital was a whorehouse.

He tested his left leg and tried to raise it slightly off the bed. The pain almost sent him back into oblivion. But he held on to consciousness and tried to bend his leg. It felt better. His muscles were stiff, his flesh was torn, and his bones were bruised. But he felt he could move on the leg, if only at a hobbling pace.

Footsteps sounded outside the door.

He closed his eyes and sank back down on the pillow.

Her perfume reached him before she did. A recognizable scent he'd inhaled many a night at the downstairs bar. It belonged to Christine Bright, the figurehead operator of the St. George. When the real manager wasn't around she was in total control. Now she was a servant, a nursemaid.

His nursemaid.

She pressed a warm wet towel against the side of his head. "Whatever happened to you shouldn't happen to anyone," she said. "Especially you, Nicky." She rinsed the towel and wiped the blood from his eye socket.

And then she gasped as his eyes snapped open. Before she could say anything he pressed his finger to his lips for silence.

"What happened?" she whispered.

"I guess I've been found out," he said.

"By who?"

Carvaggio looked at the eyes of the pretty but aging expatriate, wondering how far he could trust her. They had an easy rapport and a history of flirting that never really went anywhere. But this was different territory. It didn't matter, he realized. If not her, who could he trust?

He told her about DOA and what Liege and Priestly were really up to. About the dope plantation. Karazac and the village. About the people he was working with. And then he gave her a contact number for Hal Brognola.

"Oh, my God," she said. "What should I do?"

"Get as far away from here as possible. Get everyone else away."

"But how? Priestly's got his people all over the place. Lot of strangers. A really hard crew."

"Just get out as soon as you can. Call that number and let them know where I am. And tell them Liege is on his way. They'll come and get me if they're not on their way already. If DOA's been gathering here, they'll know it."

The woman stared at him. He was offering her a reprieve, but he was also asking her to risk her life.

"What about you?"

"I'm staying here. I can't move that much."

"You'll need something for the pain."

"No," he said. "I need something to keep me from getting any more pain."

She looked quizzically at him.

"The gun behind the bar," he said.

"You know about that?"

"I spent a lot of time watching you."

She smiled and gently touched his face.

"Get it for me?" he asked.

She nodded, then went about cleaning him up and applying a fresh bandage to his bruised face. "I wish it could have been different," she said. "You and I could have been good together."

"There's time enough when this is over."

They locked eyes. Both of them were aware that time was running out for him. He could barely move, and he was in a hotel full to capacity with hard-core mercs. "I'll be waiting for you," she said. Then she leaned over and kissed him.

THE WOODEN DUGOUTS drifted down the river toward New Albion, silently knifing toward the shore. One by one the boats landed and dropped off Felix Tomasa's Dragon Unit. They climbed up the banks and then filtered through the dark dense forest that surrounded the small town. All of the men took up positions in the forest and waited for the tour helicopter to arrive from Belize.

Shortly past midnight a bright white light appeared over the jungle canopy, rapidly growing larger as the familiar sound of whirring rotors echoed through the night air.

The pilot brought it down at the end of the street where there was just enough space for a safe approach.

Simon Liege stepped out of the chopper and hurried to the St. George Bar and Hotel.

He was halfway there when he heard the armada approaching.

It was the same kind of heavy drone he'd heard during wartime. The sound of a fleet of helicopters swooping in on the target.

He started running back toward the chopper, then realized

it would be committing suicide if he climbed back in. He dashed to the hotel, taking out his automatic pistol as he saw several shadows emerging from the river's edge.

He crashed through the front doors and saw a group of startled men sitting around tables. Some drinking, some stirring from sleep, some gaping at him. "They're here," he said. "They're coming!" He fired his pistol into the floor. The loud report echoed through the hotel, a 9 mm alarm for every merc in the house.

Several mercenaries ran out onto the second-floor landing that looked down on the main bar. They gripped the wraparound railing and looked down at Liege. The last one was Aaron Priestly, who bulled his way through the other men.

"Where the hell are the women?" Liege shouted.

Priestly looked around, trying to wipe the sleep and the whiskey from his eyes. Saw the empty bar. "Gone," he said.

"Gone," Liege repeated. "Well, gents, so are we. We're about to be hit by a fucking army, and we haven't got a single hostage to bargain with. Get the heavy weapons out and get ready for a siege."

"Wait!" Priestly shouted. "We've still got Carvaggio."

But Liege hadn't heard him. He was too busy shouting orders to the mercs, who were flipping over tables and making a barricade by the front door.

Seconds later the hotel began to shake as the special ops gunships flew low over the rooftops, rattling the windows and sending tremors throughout the rafters. It was standard psychological warfare. The deafening rotor wash sounded like drumbeats of Apocalypse for anyone caught inside the hotel. It also served another purpose, providing cover for the commandos who were abseiling silently from the helicopters down onto the roof.

CARVAGGIO WAS STANDING in the middle of the room when Priestly slammed the door halfway open.

Priestly gaped at the vacant bed as if it were the empty tomb itself. His old soldier's instinct caused him to bear down on Carvaggio as he used the open door as a shield.

Carvaggio fired first. The big revolver bucked in his hand and chewed a hole first through the wood, then through Priestly's stout chest.

Priestly gasped and then went down, literally a dead drunk once and for all.

Carvaggio glanced back at the window, considering it as a possible exit from the maelstrom.

He'd gotten out of the bed at the first sound of attack, knowing from experience that the helicopters were dropping off troops. He probably could be saved if he got to the window and waited. Or maybe some other mercs would come in and finish the job Priestly started.

Carvaggio limped to the doorway and grabbed on to the sill for support. Echoes of gunfire sounded throughout the hotel. Most of the shouting and shooting was coming from the first floor. A loud car engine was running—probably used by Brognola's troops to ram through the front door.

He went out into the hallway and started walking to the landing.

From the floor above him he heard small explosives going off, breaching entry for the commandos to drop down.

Out in the hallway he heard Liege shouting orders to his men, directing the attack. His voice could only be heard between chattering bursts from some kind of machine gun.

Carvaggio made it to the end of the hallway and then stepped out into a room to room, table to table war.

Smoke filled the bar below. Bullets crashed through shattered windows and thin wooden walls. The blunt reinforced nose of an SUV was sitting in the middle of the saloon. It was dented and pockmarked with bullets. The doors were open, and there was a dead man hanging half out of the seats.

Automatic fire zipped across the room. Belize National Police agents and Special Forces commandos were trading fire with the mercs. The DOA gunners stood their ground. They'd been on both sides of this kind of combat before and knew there was no easy way out. It was stand and fight or it was surrender. And no one in this crew was ready to surrender.

Carvaggio heard his name called from behind him. He turned back down the hallway and saw a man in black—one of the commandos who'd come to take him out of the building. "This way, this way," the man shouted.

But from the corner of his eye he saw Liege standing at the end of the second-floor railing, firing an Ameli SAW machine gun into the crowd below. The lightweight weapon had a 200-round box magazine, and half of it was spraying into Brognola's rescue force.

The bullets were arcing across the floor and drilling a path toward the stairway where Belasko was slamming a knife-wielding merc in the jaw and thumping his Beretta against the guy's chest.

It was all happening at once in that strange slow-motion combat where he saw all of the alternatives.

There was only one course to follow.

"Simon!" Carvaggio called out.

The DOA leader glanced his way, saw the revolver and swung the barrel of the Ameli toward him.

Carvaggio pulled the trigger and Liege jerked back against the wall. At the same time the barrel of the Ameli spit flame.

Something picked Carvaggio up and threw him down onto the floor, flat on his back. Fire spread through him and bullets burned the air over his head. He started to fade, thinking he made the wrong choice, thinking that true mercenaries sold their services to the highest bidder and he could have escaped death if he wanted to. But he knew it was the right choice as stillness settled him. He wasn't a mercenary. He was a soldier, serving not the highest bidder, but the highest power. He closed his eyes knowing that he was going out the right way.

BOLAN SAW the exchange as he raced up the top of the stairs. He saw Carvaggio go down as well as a wounded Liege leaning against the wall.

"Nick!" he shouted, heading for Carvaggio's bloodied body. Then he saw Liege stumble forward and rest the barrel of the machine gun on top of the railing, swiveling it at Bolan.

The Executioner dived to the floor as twenty rounds of lead chewed the wall behind him and covered him with splinters. He kept sliding across the floor with the Beretta stretched in front of him, flicking the selector to full-automatic and then turning the barrel just as he reached Carvaggio. He pulled hard on the trigger and stitched Liege from breastbone to brain.

Liege lunged forward and then tumbled down to the bar below, his dead body slamming hard against the wood.

Last call for DOA.

With Liege dead, the other mercs lost their hope and many of them lost their lives in the last few seconds of the gun battle.

A few remaining mercs threw down their weapons and dropped to the floor as the black-clad commandos trained their weapons on them.

Bolan got to his feet and stood by the body of Nicholas Carvaggio. He said a silent goodbye as he looked down at his face. For a moment it seemed as if the veteran soldier was looking back at him. Eyes open. No regrets.

Carvaggio had crossed the border that was waiting for all of them.

Don't miss the high-tech, fast-paced adventure
of title #55 of Stony Man...

Be sure to get in on the action!

DON PENDLETON'S

STONY
AMERICA'S ULTRA-COVERT INTELLIGENCE AGENCY

MAN

EXTREME MEASURES

In a brilliantly conceived plot to weaken America from
within, a renegade faction of Islamic fundamentalists
has triggered a series of terrorist attacks across the
U.S., masking their agenda by unleashing a bloodbath
in their own backyard. The terror wave is fast
approaching real time. Stony Man enters the game,
deploying state-of-the-art technology to deliver a
killing blow to America's attackers.

Available in October 2001 at your favorite retail outlet.

Or order your copy now by sending your name, address, zip or postal code, along with
a check or money order (please do not send cash) for $5.99 for each book ordered
($6.99 in Canada), plus 75¢ postage and handling ($1.00 in Canada), payable to Gold
Eagle Books, to:

In the U.S.	In Canada
Gold Eagle Books	Gold Eagle Books
3010 Walden Avenue	P.O. Box 636
P.O. Box 9077	Fort Erie, Ontario
Buffalo, NY 14269-9077	L2A 5X3

Please specify book title with your order.
Canadian residents add applicable federal and provincial taxes.

GOLD
EAGLE®

GSM55

James Axler

OUTLANDERS®

TOMB OF TIME

Now a relic of a lost civilization, the ruins of Chicago hold a cryptic mystery for Kane. In the subterranean annexes of the hidden predark military installations deep beneath the city, a cult of faceless shadow figures wields terror in submission to an unseen, maniacal god. He has lured his old enemies into a battle once again for the final and deadliest confrontation.

In the Outlands,
the shocking truth is humanity's last hope.

**In a ruined world, the past and future clash
with frightening force...**

JAMES AXLER

DEATH LANDS®

Sunchild

Ryan Cawdor and his warrior companions come face-to-face with
the descendants of a secret society who were convinced that
paradise awaited at the center of the earth. This cult is inexorably
tied to a conspiracy of twentieth-century scientists devoted to
fulfiling a vision of genetic manipulation. In this labyrinthine ville,
some of the descendants of the Illuminated Ones are pursuing the
dream of their legacy—while others are dedicated to its nightmare.

Even in the Deathlands, twisted human beliefs endure....

Available in December 2001 at your favorite retail outlet.